A Candlelight Ecstasy Romance™

IT WAS A DANGEROUS DELIGHT

The intoxicating feel of his hard body so closely
entwined with her own sapped her resistance.
Unconsciously she leaned forward, resting against him,
her blue eyes held captive by his magnetic brown ones.
Rafe's mouth lowered over hers, tasting, exploring, and
devouring her with savage abandon. The provocative
mastery of his touch spread molten fire through her
veins. . . .

A DREAM COME TRUE

Elaine Raco Chase

A CANDLELIGHT ECSTASY ROMANCE™

Published by
Dell Publishing Co., Inc.
1 Dag Hammarskjold Plaza
New York, New York 10017

Dell ® TM 681510, Dell Publishing Co., Inc.

Candlelight Ecstasy Romance™ is a trademark of
Dell Publishing Co., Inc., New York, New York.

ISBN: 0-440-11697-y

Printed in the United States of America

First printing—March 1982

Dear Reader:

In response to your continued enthusiasm for Candlelight Ecstasy Romances™, we are increasing the number of new titles from four to six per month.

We are delighted to present sensuous novels set in America, depicting modern American men and women as they confront the provocative problems of modern relationships.

Throughout the history of the Candlelight line, Dell has tried to maintain a high standard of excellence to give you the finest in reading enjoyment. That is and will remain our most ardent ambition.

Anne Gisonny
Editor
Candlelight Romances

With grateful appreciation to:
Joan Erdman
Diane McCart
Blanche VanderWende
who made moving to Florida a pleasure

CHAPTER ONE

"Surprise! Surprise!" came their breathless chorus, and Kit Forrester was.

"We've brought wine and cheese." Jeanne Peters grinned pertly at her friend, indicating the brown grocery bag she was clutching. "And after climbing up four hot flights to get to your penthouse garret, we want to hear about every second of your five romantic nights at sea."

"Maybe Kit's got the captain of the ship in there and that's why she's so reluctant to let us in," teased Nancy Billings, eyeing the still partially closed apartment door.

"The captain of the *Conquistador* is a short, balding, but terribly sweet grandfather of eight," Kit laughed good-naturedly, stepping aside as her two best friends entered her tiny attic apartment. She was momentarily taken aback by the sight of a third guest, a petite young blonde, whose model-thin body was encased in a perfectly coordinated red linen pant outfit with black reptile accessories. "Hello," she faltered, hastily trying to associate the visitor's pouty features with a name from the office steno pool.

Jeanne Peters quickly came to her rescue. "Kit, I don't think you've ever met Mr. Shippley's daughter, Marybeth. She's been handling the reception desk all week."

"I understand you work in statistics, Kit." Marybeth eyed the tall redhead with interest before gliding into the apartment. "I'm afraid I seldom get down in the basement of Daddy's building to visit that department." She raised a finely plucked eyebrow, glanced around the room, turning her small ringed hand into a fan, and gasped. "My goodness, don't tell me this itty-bitty place doesn't even have air conditioning!"

Kit, shielded from view as she closed the front door, twisted her full lips into an exaggerated grimace. "I'm afraid the circuit breakers would never tolerate an air conditioner. It barely handles my window exhaust fan," she explained in a far friendlier tone than she felt. "Why don't you and Nancy have a seat. Jeanne, you can help me turn the wine into spritzers and arrange a cheese platter."

Jeanne followed her into the small galley kitchen,

which was one step up from the living room and shielded by a long counter with shutters.

"I have just two questions," Kit hissed in a low whisper. "What is the boss's daughter doing in my living room and why were you in the office on a Sunday afternoon?"

Jeanne grinned, handed her the bottle of white wine, and opened the package of crackers. "We were asked to work this weekend to catch up on the filing and correspondence because eighty percent of the staff has been out with that miserable stomach flu, and"—her voice stalled dramatically—"to get ready for the merger."

"Merger?" Kit frowned. There had been no hint of any type of merger when she went on vacation last week.

"I know, it came as a surprise to everyone." Jeanne shook her head in disbelief. "We still don't know who will take over Shippley Electronics or if we're all going to keep our jobs. There hasn't been one bit of office gossip either," she said, pouting ruefully.

Kit handed her a knife and plate before crossing to the small refrigerator. She had been working at Shippley Electronics for the last fourteen months, since coming to San Antonio from Long Island. She had immediately fallen in love with the city and its friendly people. "I have the strangest feeling I should have banked my vacation pay this year," Kit muttered thoughtfully, taking ice cubes and a bottle of club soda from the tiny appliance. "The cruise fare would come in handy if I'm to join the ranks of the unemployed."

"I don't think you'll have any trouble getting another job, Kit," Jeanne said with total sincerity. "You're the sharpest secretary in the company. Remember how Mr. Shippley loved that component report you put together?"

Kit shrugged diffidently. "In the midst of any business dealings the employees usually end up with the worst of the deal," she cautioned speculatively. "Even with a man as fair and conscientious as Jack Shippley. After all, we're dealing with the unknown factor of a new employer."

"You might be right about that," said Jeanne, nodding dolefully. "But it's out of our hands. Just be glad you got the chance to have a super vacation and weren't in the office to catch that rotten flu bug. I was sick for five days," she groaned, rolling her eyes in remembered agony.

"Yes, I guess I was lucky to have missed that," Kit mumbled, searching intently for a bottle opener in the kitchen drawer.

"Mr. Shippley personally asked Nancy and I to come in late this afternoon, at a double-time rate of course." Jeanne grinned.

Kit laughed. "I guess that eased the pain of giving up a busy Sunday."

"You know how busy our Sundays, or for that matter our Fridays and Saturdays, have been lately."

12

The brunette grimaced. "We're counting on getting a vicarious thrill hearing about your holiday. I know you won't disappoint us."

Kit finished mixing the wine and soda, and poured it into four tall ice-filled glasses. "Why on earth would Marybeth want to hear about my vacation?" she asked curiously.

"She overheard Nancy and I talking about seeing you tonight and invited herself along. She seemed unusually interested when she heard you sailed on the *Conquistador*'s maiden voyage. I haven't the faintest idea why—"

She was interrupted by Nancy's voice calling from the living room. "Are you two ever coming out? We're parched."

"Here we are," Kit called, quickly adding a lime garnish to the glasses and heading back into the living room with Jeanne in tow. She set the heavy tray on a white wicker trunk that doubled as a coffee table. "I understand you're interested in hearing about the cruise." Kit smiled graciously and handed Marybeth a tall frosted glass.

"That's right," the blonde drawled slowly, pausing to take a long sip of the refreshing liquid. "My older sister, Tracy, was to have sailed on the ship with her ... well ... he is practically her fiancé. They had another one of their little tiffs and Tracy went off in a huff with our mama to New York City to see the new fall fashions. She's going to be just green when I tell her one of Daddy's employees made the cruise and she missed it." Marybeth finished on a tone that held more than a trace of malice and sibling rivalry. "However did you manage to secure a cabin? The maiden voyage of the ship was filled with the Lone Star's finest," she added with a condescending smile.

Kit glanced from Nancy to Jeanne with a hint of deviltry lurking in her light blue eyes. "I'm afraid that even the cream of the Texas crop drew the line at a small inside cabin on the seventh deck of a seven-deck ship," she returned dryly before seating herself in a wicker rocker that matched the one Marybeth occupied.

"You know," Nancy mused, eyeing Kit's lithe but shapely figure in a clingy white terry jump suit, "I thought for sure you'd gain weight. I understand they serve mountains of food on cruise ships, but you look like you lost a few pounds."

Kit quickly swallowed a gulp of spritzer and cleared her throat. "Like I said, there were seven decks to investigate, two swimming pools, lots of activities. I just seemed to work off their fantastic food offerings."

"That's true. After all, who'd want to sit and eat all day when there was so much to do?" Jeanne said, bobbing her head in agreement. "Now, don't leave out one single detail."

"Okay, okay." Kit laughed obligingly. "The bus ride from San Anton to Galveston Bay was not memorable. The sight of the S.S. *Conquistador* was. You just can't imagine how big that ship is. Seven decks, three lounges, a disco, a gambling casino, coffee shops, two dining rooms, a shopping arcade, theater, two swimming pools, a sun deck, sauna, exercise spa—it was a floating village!"

Both Jeanne and Nancy gasped in amazement as Kit continued. "My cabin was very small. Luckily it was one of the few single rooms, so that made it seem larger. It was a sunny yellow with orange and green accents, small bath, closet, and dresser. Everything very efficient and compact."

"Not unlike your own apartment," Marybeth interrupted in her flat, lazy nasal voice, causing the others to roll their eyes in silent condemnation.

"That's true," Kit agreed dryly. "At any rate, the sailing was just like in the movies. Lots of streamers, confetti, and horns. We were all crowded on the various open decks waving to anybody while the newspaper photographers snapped their cameras. Then the ship headed for the island of Cozumel on the Yucatán coast of Mexico."

"What's Cozumel like?" Nancy interjected hastily.

"Cozumel is beautiful. White sands, emerald water, lots of boutiques featuring native Mayan clothes, coral, jewelry, and handicrafts. It was our only port of call and our only source of solid land."

"Don't tell me you got seasick," Nancy chided her friend.

"Don't be silly," Jeanne interrupted. "Kit's got a cast-iron stomach. Anybody who can wolf down all the Tex-Mex food she does couldn't possibly get seasick. Right, Kit?"

Kit opened her mouth, closed it, cleared her throat, and smiled. "Right. Although I have to admit the world of a cruise ship is always slightly at an angle."

"What did you do the four days you were at sea?" Nancy asked. "I bet there were lots of parties and things. Did you go into the casino?"

"I can just hear the mariachi serenade drifting over the salt air as you strolled along the deck watching the moonlight dancing on the sea," Jeanne gushed dreamily.

"Well—"

"Kit, you must have met someone." Jeanne stopped and closely inspected her friend. "My gosh. Look at her blush! She did meet someone!"

"Now wait a minute," Kit managed hastily, trying unsuccessfully to stop the surge of color that again invaded her cheeks.

"Kit, for heaven's sake, why try to deny it?" Nancy chimed in. "This is just what we were hoping would happen. You meeting someone exciting on your glamorous adventure at sea. Jeanne and I have already decided to book a cruise on our vacation."

"Absolutely," Jeanne concurred. "I'm just ecstatic that you met someone. Now, what's he like? Oh, I bet he's tall, tanned, and handsome, right?" At the sight of her friend's crimson face, she squealed in delight.

16

"Kit, I will scream if you don't say something," Nancy said firmly, grabbing the redhead's arm impatiently.

Kit coughed nervously, extricated her arm, and reached for a slice of cheese. Her mind whirled in four directions at once. Her eyes caught the keen interest on Marybeth's face and the anxious features of her two friends. She was trapped. Her gaze settled on a macho cigarette ad on the back of one of the magazines that were stacked next to her rocking chair. "You're right, he is tall, but of course I need someone over six feet." She laughed lightly. "He's got dark hair and eyes, a rugged face and muscular build. He plays a lot of sports and, of course, was very bronzed by the sun."

"How did you meet him?" Jeanne interrupted, completely entranced with Kit's good luck.

"Well, we just kept running into each other on the ship, started talking, and ended up . . . partners for the cruise," Kit said in a rush, then sat back, extremely pleased with herself at the way she had worded that description.

"It was fate. Imagine, being with someone like that both *day* and *night,*" Nancy fantasized enviously. "It's like being engaged."

"Well, er . . ."

"When are you going to see him again? Is he from San Antonio?"

"Well, I certainly—"

"What's his name?" asked Marybeth in a voice high and commanding in its tone.

"His name?" Kit blinked, surprised that she'd even ask.

"Yes, Kit, tell us his name," chorused her two friends in an earnest appeal to have all the facts.

She gulped a mouthful of her drink, trying desperately to refocus her creative talents on this new problem. "His name is Morgan . . . Raphael Morgan," her voice announced in an unbelievably calm tone. She was so busy fingering the bobbing ice cubes in her glass and trying not to blush, she completely missed the look of shock and astonishment that crossed Marybeth Shippley's previously bored features.

"Raphael Morgan." Jeanne savored the name slowly. "That sounds just like a name out of one of those romance novels I always read."

"If you all would excuse me"—Marybeth jumped up suddenly, handing her empty glass to a startled Kit—"I must be running along. I had no idea just how late it was getting."

"Certainly," Kit muttered hastily, shrugging her shoulders in puzzlement. "It was nice to finally meet you."

"Well, I will be seeing you again next Saturday night, when Daddy has a little cocktail party for his employees. I'm sure it will prove most surprising." She smiled slyly before undulating out the door.

"What on earth was that all about?" Nancy frowned.

"I can't imagine." Jeanne shrugged. "Maybe we were boring her. After all, I'm sure the Shippleys have gone on cruises before, and we certainly aren't in her circle of friends."

"I'm not sure I'd want to be," Kit said evenly, staring intently at the closed door. "I have the feeling Marybeth lives with snobbery and money as her defense against good manners."

"She is also the biggest gossip I've ever met," Nancy complained. "She's been subbing for Mae on reception and I really believe she listens in on the phone calls. Luckily, this is her last week."

Kit settled herself in the wicker rocker. "Have you ever met Sister Tracy?" she asked her two companions.

Both girls shook their heads. "Tracy's never been into the office and didn't even attend the barbecue last year. I think Marybeth likes to get all the exposure she can, and that's why she subs in the office," Nancy added with due consideration.

"I'm glad I'm stuck in the basement of Daddy's building." Kit mimicked the departed girl's drawl perfectly, causing them all to succumb to peals of laughter.

"Now, we want to hear about everything that happened on board your own 'love boat' all over again," Jeanne said firmly, handing Kit her empty glass for a refill.

Kit was mentally exhausted by the time her two friends left a little after ten. Mechanically, she tidied up the small living room, quickly turned the sofa into a bed, and wandered into the oversize closet that led to a small bathroom. Kit stripped off her jump suit and pulled a light cotton nightshirt over her head. Her eyes caught sight of the five-foot-ten, one-hundred-thirty-five-pound, red-haired *liar* reflected in the full-length mirror on the door.

Like a magnet, her image pulled her closer for an intense scrutiny. Time hadn't changed her over the years. She had attained her lofty altitude at the early age of twelve. It had taken years of exercise to correct the hump shoulders of poor posture she had adopted to disguise her height. The long, wavy hair was still the bright copper color of her youth. There was nothing dainty and delicate about the strong features, straight nose, and generous mouth. The only time she ever had cheekbones was when she ate something sour. Her best feature was her eyes. Wide and almond-shaped, they were an unusual shade of light blue and looked naive and innocent even when telling the most outrageous lies.

Sister Cecilia, headmistress at St. Lukes, just one of the many schools she had been sent to, had often thrown up her hands and shaken her head in despair over Kit Forrester, who told the most fanciful tales of why her homework was never done. In order to know with absolute certainty who put what frog, snake, or firecracker in what desk, Sister Cecilia needed to look no further than to the wide-eyed, innocent-looking, at times even angelic, totally undisciplined tomboy who plagued the school for three years.

Kit leaned closer, staring at the impassive portrait the mirror reflected. She wondered if eyes were truly the mirrors of the soul. Her soul was riddled with lies. She had always lied, especially to herself, creating and living in a dream world because her own world had been so ugly. Now she was still lying, even in her new world.

"You'll never change," Kit hissed out loud at her reflection, then roughly pushed open the door and stalked back to the living room, plopping herself on the sofa bed. She had thought wisdom would come with age, hoping the professional veneer she had adopted over the years would successfully overcome the lying days of her youth. This time she had really outdone herself, making one small lie go a long, long way. Her blue eyes rolled heavenward. She had the feeling Sister Cecilia knew it too!

Kit had embarked on her cruise with visions of the most exciting vacation possible. A gift to herself for all the years spent dreaming of twinkling stars on moonlit seas, soft trade winds ruffling her hair, and, perhaps, a romance with a tall, handsome man under a tropical sky. But they were dreams, lofty dreams, that had crashed into the sea.

The only people who had shared her five-day cruise were the sixty-year-old ship's doctor and his nurse-wife. She had spent four out of the five days confined to her small, inside, seventh-deck cabin, suffering from a combination of stomach flu and one of the worst cases of seasickness the doctor had ever seen.

The trip had started off with great expectations. She had boarded the ship, quickly unpacked a rather glamorous array of clothes she had recklessly purchased, then set out to explore, deck by deck. The *Conquistador* had been everything she had told Jeanne and Nancy. Its sheer size and luxury were enough to take your breath away. Then, once clear of Galveston Bay, her new world at a permanent tilt and with no stable horizon to focus on, she had begun to feel queasy, headachy, and green with nausea.

She tried lying down on a deck chair, eyes closed, inhaling the fresh salt air. When that failed, she scurried to her room and tried resting in her cabin. Getting no relief and feeling worse every second, Kit had called for the ship's physician. Dr. Martinez and his wife, Isabelle, had been most kind. He found she had a fever and swollen glands. Kit recognized that they were the same symptoms her office workers had reported when they were hit with the flu. Isabelle had kindly supplied her with magazines and paperbacks and had kept her company.

The medication only made Kit feel extremely groggy. She had actually slept for most of the trip, even missing the visit to Cozumel. Luckily, the ship's shopping arcade provided her with a few souvenirs and brochures to bring home.

Her vacation had turned into five days of sleep and nausea on a luxury liner. Kit let out a long, disgusted groan. The worst part was lying to Nancy and Jeanne. Why had she ever done such a thing? It wasn't just to save face because Marybeth Shippley had shown up unexpectedly. Kit knew she was capable of turning the whole awful cruise into a joke. No, her reasons ran much deeper than that.

Jeanne, Nancy, and Kit were basically alike. They had all come from broken homes. They were all intelligent, attractive women. Jeanne, with her dark hair and eyes, petite figure and pert face; Nancy, an average-size blonde with a bubbly personality; and herself. They were all twenty-five, they were all secretaries in the same office, and they were all seeking the one thing they lacked during their childhood years—love.

All three were new to Texas, coming to San Antonio fourteen months ago and meeting at Shippley Electronics. They had formed a fast friendship, using one another as the families they never had. To their chagrin, they found that female self-reliance had its limitations.

At first glance, there seemed to be an abundance of male companions—at the office, community tennis and recreational centers, and the very respectable singles bars and discos that heavily populated the area. There were a lot of potential dates, but after a variety of similar happenings to all the girls, they were far more willing to turn down invitations these days than handle verbal and, sometimes, physical matches at the end of an evening when the men in their own age group expected a quick trip to bed in repayment for a cover charge and two drinks!

Kit had been waiting all her life for someone to love her. But each step seemed frought with discouragement and despair. Much of her upbringing had been in schools. She had lain awake, weeping in the dark over the sins that had sent her to the cold, sterile, shallow institutions full of discipline and lacking in warmth and love. She had built up hurt shields during her growing years and carried them through to adulthood.

As she matured, she packaged herself in false wrappings, developing a protective steel mask over an eggshell demeanor. She appeared cool and competent, carefree and self-reliant, giving the illusion her life was under control. It didn't always work. The anxieties of the past seemed to encroach on the present, and she often fell victim to her own insecurities.

Kit rested her chin on updrawn knees, wondering why she had never been loved. You need to be perfect, she thought glumly. Wear the right perfume and the right size and style of dress, say the right things, have the right friends. The perfect storybook heroine—petite in size, rosebud mouth, heart-shaped face, breathless voice—the girl whose head barely reaches the hero's heart. No, that wasn't her.

It might be easier to settle for sex. At twenty-five, Kit felt mature enough to handle sex. The trouble was, she didn't want sex. While she had grown physically and chronologically, emotionally she was still stunted. Too many memories had soiled every attempt she had ever made to relax and get close to a man. She longed for a man to have a caring relationship with, not just to be used in a physical act.

She rolled over on her stomach and pulled the magazine with the cigarette ad onto her pillow. The dark-haired man who grinned back at her was very attractive, and he certainly had come in very handy when she needed a description tonight. But where on earth had she come up with that name—Raphael Morgan? Kit frowned thoughtfully, her smooth forehead puckering in concentration. She associated the name with the *Conquistador*. It could have been a steward or a waiter. She had read so many brochures and magazines while confined to her cabin that in all probability she had put two names together and invented Raphael Morgan.

Her long fingers lightly caressed the printed picture with more than a hint of longing. It would have been wonderful to meet someone like him on a cruise. She had promised herself to be a little less cool and aloof, to change the path of her life and be more outgoing and aggressive. A cruise into the *joie de vivre*—the zestful enjoyment of life. Could she have done it? To be honest, no. Despite her Amazonian proportions, she was still fragile and unsure of herself.

Kit reached up, snapped off the light, and punched

her pillow. Her only salvation was the fact that the merger would be the number-one topic of conversation at work. Her little romantic escapade at sea would die a quick, clean death. If anyone asked her about the mysterious Raphael Morgan, she could easily invent another lie, sending him back into the depths of her imagination. She yawned sleepily and drifted off into blissful slumber.

CHAPTER TWO

"Isn't this place fabulous," gushed Jeanne Peters to her two companions standing out on the lighted balcony of Jack Shippley's twentieth-floor condominium. Below, the gentle refrain of a mariachi serenade drifted from one of the waterborne restaurants on the tranquil San Antonio River.

"I think I like their ranch better," Kit said with due consideration, looking back through the open French doors that gave a full view of the pastel color scheme and the elegant Georgian furnishings. Most of the firm's salaried personnel were milling around the spacious apartment, all enjoying the lavish cocktail and hors d'oeuvres party that their employer was giving.

"You city girls always long for country life,"

Nancy Billings teased. "Jeanne and I grew up on farms in the Midwest, and this is heaven," she stated emphatically, spreading her arms wide.

"We never get the chance to wear such glamorous dresses at the Labor Day barbecue at their ranch," Jeanne reminded them, giving a quick pirouette to show off her own pale lemon chiffon halter dress.

"You're right about that," Kit conceded. "I wish I could wear such a lovely shade of red, Nancy."

Nancy beamed. "This little gem cost half a week's salary. I thought I'd never get a chance to wear it," she told them, fingering the lacy peasant embroidery on the vibrant bodice. "But if there's one person who is turning heads tonight, it's you, Kit."

"For a while I thought I was paranoid," Kit admitted, remembering the odd, penetrating looks she had been getting all evening. "Mr. Shippley and Marybeth, especially, seem to be watching me. I get the feeling they're all waiting for something to happen."

The three of them walked back into the apartment, stopping to refill their punch glasses and peruse the canapé selection.

"Well, you look stunning," Jeanne told her, popping a shrimp puff into her amber-tinted mouth. "I love your new hairstyle, and that dress is divine. You've been different ever since you came back from that cruise. If you weren't my best friend, I'd hate you!"

Kit laughed and turned to refill her punch cup.

Her blue eyes caught sight of her reflection in the silver bowl. With all humility, even her distorted, frosted image looked striking. The *new* Kit was courtesy of the New You, a beauty salon that had just opened on the Paseo del Rio. She had discovered the salon on her lunch hour while window-shopping along the two-mile stretch of boutiques and cafés that lined the San Antonio River. On impulse she had made an appointment for this morning.

Kit had panicked halfway through the haircut, but Mr. Charles, the shop's owner, deftly calmed her nerves, layered her hair, and shampooed in a henna pack. Her previously unruly mane now flowed into controlled, burnished waves to her shoulders. Kit had succumbed to a free makeup lesson, watching as the cosmetician's slightly heavier hand with color and shadows brought her blue eyes, bone structure, and mouth into companionable alliance. Her slim, teal blue dress with its low, draped neckline had been purchased for the cruise, and she was glad to have a chance to wear it.

The overall effect was a metamorphosis that boosted her ego. For possibly the first time in her life, she didn't feel gawky and awkward.

"That's what being in love does for you," she heard Nancy sigh. "All the girls in the steno pool have decided to book cruises, hoping to repeat your luck and come back engaged."

Engaged! Kit choked on a piece of cheese. The office gossip mill had certainly been working overtime embellishing her own fictitious romance way out of proportion. Her hope of having the impending merger overshadow her trip had been a false one. She stared at her image in the punch bowl, watching her soft, sensuous reflection melt away into an ugly, blemished portrait. How could she have lied and deceived her friends? She had to make immediate restitution, salvage what she could of her self-esteem and make a full confession. Kit took a hefty swallow of the potent rum punch, feeling the need for a little Dutch courage as she came to a most difficult decision.

"Listen, Jeanne, Nancy." Kit cleared her throat. "Why don't we go back out on the patio? I've got a little story to tell you. It's really quite funny." She gave a weak laugh.

"I'm not budging one inch," Jeanne said suddenly, quickly snapping her body to attention. "Look at the gorgeous man Marybeth is leading across the living room. She's certainly playing the roll of hostess to the hilt while her mother and sister are still in New York."

"Maybe he'll turn out to be a relative and she'll introduce him to us," Nancy said hopefully, her eyes following the couple's slow progress across the crowded room.

Kit put the crystal cup down, wearily rubbing her forehead, glad her back hid from view the uneasy tension showing on her attractive face. "This really is important," she said urgently.

"Nothing can be more important than a potential introduction to the tall, dark-haired, handsome man who just brought the party to life," Jeanne said firmly. "He's even got a mustache." She gave a low ecstatic groan.

"Do us a favor, Kit," Nancy hissed, as the couple drew nearer, "scrunch down and don't turn around. You've already found a man. We want the same opportunity."

Kit exhaled slowly. She'd just have to tell them the truth later when they drove her home. If she explained everything honestly, she could only hope their friendship wouldn't be jeopardized. It would have been so much easier to tell the truth right at the beginning instead of weaving such a tangled web of lies.

Marybeth Shippley's flat nasal voice sliced into her troubled thoughts. "Well, here he is, Kit," she drawled, a sarcastic quality evident in her tone. "I told you the evening would hold a few surprises."

Kit slowly turned and found herself staring into a handsome, mustached face. The man was in his mid-thirties, tall, with thick side-parted wavy dark hair and twinkling brown eyes. His rugged physique was clad in an impeccably tailored dark evening suit. His intense gaze suddenly took on a devilish glint that roamed slowly over her puzzled features and lingered for tantalizing seconds on the rounded cleavage bared by the slender strapped dress.

His white teeth flashed into a wide, dimpled grin

31

and Kit began to feel very uncomfortable, a surge of color staining her cheeks. A pair of strong hands reached out, grabbed her shoulders, and imprisoned her against a broad, muscular chest. She only had time to utter a startled squeak before his mouth came down hard, parting hers. She was quite powerless to move and the stranger took his time, molding her body close against his rugged length.

He lifted his mouth from hers, still holding her captive in a steellike embrace. "Darling, what did you expect after being apart for a whole week?" he said in his deep masculine drawl.

The stunned look on Kit's face was equaled only by the shock registered on Jeanne's, Nancy's, and even Marybeth's! She swallowed convulsively but couldn't seem to find her voice.

The stranger's voice, however, was rich with amusement. "I guess I'll just have to introduce myself. I'm Rafe Morgan. I understand Kit's told you all about *us.*"

Kit's mouth dropped and she felt her stomach heave, especially when she noticed the taunting gleam in Rafe Morgan's dark eyes. Luckily her reaction went unnoticed by her friends, who were starry-eyed with his introduction.

Jeanne was the first to speak. "Well, this is certainly a surprise. We had no idea you'd be here. Kit didn't mention it." She gave her friend a disapproving glance.

"Well, now, don't blame Kit," Rafe said with a

broad smile. "It was all Marybeth's doing. When she called and told me that my"—he hesitated slightly—"fiancée was an employee of her father's and would be here tonight, I just couldn't stay away." He gave Kit a quick hug. "That's one thing my little Kit never mentioned when we were on the ship together."

His 'little Kit' suddenly felt her knees buckle, and the only thing that kept her from hitting the peach carpeting was Rafe Morgan's arm locked tightly around her waist. The whole scene had a touch of unreality about it, and for possibly the first time in her life, Kit Forrester couldn't think of any explanation for this ghastly turn of events. The lover she had so conveniently invented had suddenly turned into a six-foot-two-inch, flesh-and-blood male, with considerable virile magnetism, if she interpreted the looks on her friend's faces correctly.

Marybeth's sharp tone brought her wandering thoughts back with a jolt. "You can imagine how shocked I was when Kit mentioned your name last week while telling us about the cruise," she said, smiling slyly and brushing a strand of hair off her bare shoulders.

Kit focused a piercing, icy blue gaze on the petite blonde in the black strapless taffeta hostess gown that was enlivened with threads of fuchsia and gold. Marybeth's mouth was a thin strip of color against alabaster skin, her green eyes intently focused on Rafe Morgan's face.

33

Suddenly, Kit wondered just how factual this entire introduction really was. Her nerves were given an angry shot of adrenaline, and she was finally able to form a coherent sentence with her dry tongue. "This really was quite a surprise, Marybeth." She laughed artificially. "I'm sure you'll excuse . . . uh . . . Rafe and me, if we wander out to the patio for a few minutes." Kit grabbed his arm and all but pulled him out on the lighted balcony, leaving her friends wide-eyed and stammering at her abrupt exit.

She quickly closed the French doors, turned, squared her shoulders, and drew herself up to her full and most intimidating height. "All right, buster, hand over your wallet," Kit ordered sharply, holding out her palm.

His dark brow arched quizzically.

"There's no way on earth you can possibly be Raphael Morgan," Kit sneered, growing more and more confident by the minute. "I don't know what kind of scheme you and Marybeth have cooked up or the reason for it, but I refuse to be the brunt of the joke." She tapped the toe of her narrow-heeled black sandal impatiently. "The wallet," she repeated forcefully.

He shrugged his broad shoulders, reached into the inside pocket of his evening jacket, and handed her a slim leather billfold.

Kit flipped it open and began sorting through the various pieces of identification. Unfortunately, from the pictured driver's license to an assorted group of credit and membership cards, everything seemed to agree: he definitely was Raphael Morgan! There was a photograph of three young children, two girls and a boy, and she instantly seized a hopeful notion that he was married.

"Your children?" Kit asked, trying to avoid his amused gaze.

"My nieces and nephew," he said and grinned in reply. He straightened up from the balcony rail and crossed over to the dejected copper-haired figure. "I'm a bachelor, but I seem to have acquired a mysterious fiancée on the cruise."

"You mean *you* were on the *Conquistador*?" Kit was getting that awful sensation of nausea again. She handed back his wallet and turned away. "This is just incredible. It's just unbelievable. It's horrible . . ." Her voice trailed away in despair.

"I don't know," Rafe said considerately, sliding his arms around her slender waist. "I think it could be most enjoyable," he murmured, his warm lips nuzzling the fragrant skin at the nape of her neck.

"Will you stop that!" Kit hissed, her voice sounding jerky as she pulled away. "I realize I've got a lot of explaining to do." She gave a high, nervous laugh. "You're really going to think this is so funny when you hear—"

The patio doors flew open, revealing the stocky figure of Jack Shippley. "Well, now, here's where you two have gone and hidden yourselves."

35

"Can you blame me, Jack?" Rafe asked, slipping his arm back around Kit's waist and locking her tightly against his side. "Who wouldn't want to be alone with such a beautiful lady?"

Kit pasted a tight smile on her face before looking at her employer. "Seeing Rafe was such a . . . surprise," she managed on a slightly overstrung note, fidgeting nervously as his caressing hand began to have a chaotic effect on her body.

"Well, you can imagine my surprise when my daughter told me how you two met on that cruise," Jack said, grinning at the two of them. "Why didn't you tell him you worked for me, Kit?"

She coughed and cleared her throat. "Somehow the subject just never came up."

Rafe laughed and flashed a wide smile at the ruddy-faced man. "Who wants to talk shop in all that moonlight?"

"You've got a point there, boy." Jack laughed in return. "Although I suppose it's just a matter of semantics who works for whom."

"Now, Jack," Rafe hurriedly interjected, "I thought you had a rule about mixing business and pleasure."

Kit, anxious to find any way to extricate herself from Rafe's commanding presence, pounced on the word *business* like a lifeline. "Listen." She laughed lightly, removing the muscular arm that was still holding her. "Don't let me stop any business discussions. I'll just leave you two alone." She smiled graciously at the two men before escaping into the relative safety of the apartment.

Kit fled into the pastel blue powder room, collapsing on a padded bench in the mirrored alcove. She looked at her white, strained reflection, then closed her eyes in despair. It was like stepping into the twilight zone. How could this have possibly happened? She had invented Rafe Morgan—or thought she had. Unfortunately, he existed. Oh, God, did he ever exist, she groaned out loud. Tall, strong, commanding, his grinning mustached face loomed with three-dimensional accuracy next to hers in the mirror. She quickly averted her eyes, groping in her small clutch bag for a compact, lipstick, and comb, trying to compose herself and rationally figure a way out of this situation. Her peaceful respite was suddenly invaded by an unusually agitated Marybeth Shippley.

"Well, I just couldn't believe it till I saw it with my own two eyes," the tiny blonde exploded without preamble. "The whole idea of you and Rafe Morgan together is absolutely outrageous!"

"Really?" Kit raised a burnished arched brow.

"Do you think you'd have stood any chance at all if Tracy had been aboard that cruise ship?" Marybeth spat furiously.

Kit frowned. "What does your sister have to do with this?"

The volatile blonde gave a rather horselike snort.

"Whom do you think Rafe was practically engaged to?"

Kit gave a silent groan. "Tracy?"

"That's right," Marybeth drawled sarcastically. "We've been trying to corral him ever since he came to San Anton."

"Is this a joint effort, or are you two sisters at war over the man?" Kit questioned dryly.

Twin spots of color stained Marybeth's porcelain face. "That's none of your damn business," she hissed. "If you think you're going to walk away with him, you're in for a double-barreled fight. There's no way in hell we are going to lose him to the likes of you."

Kit's well-modulated voice was low and forceful, taking on added strength as she rose from the bench and towered over a suddenly acquired rival. "It seems to me you two have been less than successful where Rafe is concerned. If Tracy meant anything at all to him, do you honestly imagine any other woman could have interfered with that relationship?" She spoke in the most confident tone imaginable.

"We're not finished with you yet," Marybeth warned icily, and with a rustle of taffeta, quickly left the close confines of the lavatory.

Kit ran a hand through her thick copper hair. For a brief second she felt sorry for Rafe Morgan. It seemed the Shippley women were after him the way a hunter set out to bag a prize trophy. The romantic interlude she had invented was to have a far more reaching effect on her life than she could have ever imagined.

She now had Rafe Morgan and the Shippleys to contend with. Kit rolled her eyes at her reflection and grimaced. *Well, kid, you've done it again.* She squared her shoulders and took a deep breath. Whatever happened, she'd take her lumps with the confidence born of past adventures, but she wasn't about to run scared of any of them! Some sixth sense told her that Sister Cecilia was once again offering prayers in her name.

"You're just in time to hear Mr. Shippley's announcement," Jeanne whispered quietly in her left ear when she rejoined her friends in the living room.

"You certainly spent a long time on the patio with Rafe," Nancy hissed in her right ear. "I really don't blame you; he's just adorable."

Kit gave her a tight smile, which abruptly faded when she encountered Rafe's amused expression leveled at her from across the room. She hastily unlocked her gaze from his and made a supreme effort to concentrate on Jack Shippley's speech.

"I want you all to know that the rumors of a merger are true," her employer's booming voice rang out, immediately ending any further conversations. "Your positions will be secure with the new company, as will all benefits and salary levels. I had hoped to be able to introduce you all to your new boss, but that will have to remain secret just a little bit longer. Now, everyone, drink up and enjoy the party. The night's still young." Jack laughed and led a group of executives toward the bar.

A large hand settled on Kit's bare shoulder, turning her around. "I'm afraid *your* party's over," Rafe said in his deep voice. "Do you have a car?"

She shook her head. "I came with Jeanne and Nancy," she told him, indicating her two friends, who had strayed back to the buffet table.

"I doubt they'll be surprised that you're leaving with me. Go say your good-byes and I'll meet you at the elevator," he ordered in a tone she instinctively knew would tolerate no defiance.

Kit was slightly chagrined by her companion's and her employer's ready acceptance of her early departure. Minutes later she was sliding into the front seat of an opulent silver Mercedes bearing the license plate MORGAN-1. She gave Rafe the directions to her apartment, trying to relax in the air-conditioned comfort of the big car.

It was a futile attempt. Her mind was busily engaged in thinking of a variety of explanations that would extricate her from this wholly embarrassing situation. Kit shot a sidelong glance at her quiet companion, only to find that the low dash lights cast a harsh glow on his previously amused features. She meditatively gnawed her lower lip. He wasn't going to be as easy to handle as the school officials and the nuns had been. Although, she reflected brightly, tears and humility usually worked wonders in any situation!

Rafe deftly slid the powerful car into a parking spot in front of her building and followed Kit into the aging wooden structure. The staircase provided them with a sweltering, oppressive climb. Rafe had removed his dinner jacket and tie by the second level, rolled up his sleeves and unbuttoned his pleated evening shirt by the time they finally reached the attic apartment. The rush of hot, stale air that greeted them did little to cool the electrically charged atmosphere.

"Why don't you take a seat," Kit said nervously, switching on the ceiling light and gesturing toward the sofa. "I'll turn on the fan and get you a cold drink."

"Make it a tall one," Rafe ordered bluntly. He tossed his jacket on the wicker rocker and stood looking around the small room. He ducked his head under the sharply angled walls when the only other door in the room proved to be the closet that led to a dormer bath. "Is this it?" he asked, frowning and settling his tall frame on the couch.

Kit had quickly filled a tall glass with ice and lemonade and returned to the living room. "This is *my* home," she answered defiantly, her light blue eyes challenging his probing brown ones.

"Where's the bedroom?"

"You're sitting on it."

"That's convenient." The twinkle was back in his eyes. She handed him the drink and took the seat next to him, rationalizing that it would be less of a strain not to have a direct line of vision to his obviously potent charm.

"Well?" There was more than a hint of amusement in his deep voice.

How galling. She wiggled uncomfortably. "I don't know where to start."

"Try the middle."

Kit stared straight ahead, coughed, cleared her throat, and coughed again. She didn't need to pretend tears; instant regret washed over her, causing her shoulders to slump and her voice to take on a dejected tone. "I carefully saved every penny I could and was lucky enough to get a cabin on the *Conquistador*. Unfortunately, less than a day out at sea, I came down with the stomach flu that had attacked most of our office. That and being seasick provided me with a thrilling five-day cruise in my cabin." She licked her lips and turned toward Rafe, hoping to make him understand. "On my first night back home, my two friends, the ones you met tonight . . . they . . . they stopped in and wanted to hear all about my glamorous adventure on the high seas, so . . ." Her voice trailed off.

"So you gave them magic tropical romantic nights with embellishments," Rafe finished dryly. "How did you happen to pick me for a partner?"

Kit flushed, reached over to the end table, and pulled out the magazine. "I wasn't describing you," she told him in acute discomfort. "It was him," she said and pointed to the cigarette ad.

42

"You used my name," he returned crisply, tossing the magazine aside with only a vague glance.

Kit's head snapped up. "That was an accident, I swear," she said fervently, clutching his well-muscled forearm in an earnest appeal. "I thought I put your name together from some of the circulars on the ship. Honest, I really thought I had invented you."

"That's probably where you did get my name."

"Why would your name be included with the ship's personnel?" She frowned, totally bewildered by his admission.

Rafe favored her with another one of his captivating dimpled smiles. "Who do you think owns the *Conquistador*?"

"You." It came out as a low moan.

He nodded.

Abruptly, she recalled the odd way Mr. Shippley had declined to announce the company's new owner and hesitantly voiced a new fear. "You're taking over Shippley Electronics, aren't you?" she whispered thickly.

He gave her another grin and nodded again. Kit closed her eyes and groaned miserably. Rafe's finger traced the soft line of her flushed cheek down to the pulsating cord on the side of her neck, sending a sensual message coursing through her body that hastily sent Kit sliding across the cushion out of reach. "I've got to admit you are a very clever woman," he said in his deep voice, heavily laced with cynical amusement. "You must have known

43

Marybeth would contact me and that I would seek you out." He leaned further over her, pushing her against the arm of the sofa with his powerful body.

Kit gasped at his blatant innuendo. She spread her hands flat against his powerful chest, pushing him back toward the other side of the sofa with all her considerable strength. "Why, you conceited, self-centered, arrogant—" She bit off the sentence angrily. "Do you seriously think I'd make up such a story just to get your attention? I didn't even know you existed!" she snapped furiously. "What about you? Why did you go along with this when you have Tracy Shippley?" she demanded and triumphantly saw the startled expression on his face.

"Who told you about Tracy?" he countered, his dark eyes narrowing suspiciously.

"Marybeth," Kit returned quickly, savoring her sudden advantage. "She said the two of you had another one of your little spats and that's why Tracy wasn't on the cruise, sharing your cabin. She also said you two are practically engaged," she finished with sardonic glee.

"I seem to have a penchant for acquiring fiancées lately" was his oblique response.

"Well, you can get rid of me easily enough," Kit told him sharply, her mind sparking with sudden creativity.

"Oh?"

"Just tell everyone you've changed your mind. Say the sea air clouded your brain and after being back on dry land you suddenly saw the error of your ways," she told him with a self-satisfied smirk, mentally congratulating herself on how easily she'd resolved the entire situation.

"Really." Rafe said the word with slow consideration, letting his eyes roam over her features and the tumble of copper hair. "And then what? Have you sue me for breach of promise and alienation of affection?" he charged, pushing himself up from the sofa.

Kit reeled back against the cushions as if she'd been slapped. "What are you talking about!" she gasped. "We've never been affectionate! Wait just one minute," she shouted, jumping off the couch after him. She gave a startled cry when the narrow heel of her shoe caught the edge of the rag rug, throwing her off balance.

Rafe turned and managed to rescue her from what could have been a nasty fall, his large, capable hands spanning her waist while she attempted to regain her balance and composure.

"Thank you," she breathed, and tossing her head back, she looked into his face. Her forehead creased in confusion at the odd expression in his brown eyes. She saw his gaze shift from her to the view of the tiny apartment beyond. Mesmerized, she didn't balk when he pulled her close. The musky scent of his cologne assailed her senses. She realized that from his height he could see down the front of her dress. She shifted her body, an embarrassed flush again invading her face. "What are you going to do?" Kit asked in a jerky gulp.

Rafe's eyes focused on her softly parted lips. "Right now, I'm going to kiss my new fiancée good night," he murmured before his mouth hungrily sampled the sweetness of hers. The compelling attraction of this man seemed to draw a most willing response, which sent a shiver of pure physical awareness down her spine.

When Kit opened her eyes, she was standing alone in the center of the room trying to control her erratic breathing and pounding heart.

CHAPTER THREE

The hot cement sidewalk received a steady, cool drip of ice cream from Kit's cone while she walked back from the Laundromat to her apartment. The July heat had driven most of the people to the community pool or to the indoor comfort of air conditioning.

The Laundromat was part of her normal Sunday routine, which Kit had extended through late afternoon, seeking respite from the constantly ringing telephone that she stubbornly refused to answer. Emotionally, she felt ill equipped to handle a conversation with Rafe Morgan, and she didn't know what to tell Nancy and Jeanne.

The toe of her flat sandals kicked a stone from her path, and she transferred the heavy laundry bag to her other shoulder. She had tossed and turned most of the night, trying to solve this dilemma. She was still without an answer.

Kit sighed, then looked up and blinked in surprise, shading her eyes at the sight of a yellow moving van parked in front of her corner apartment building. When she had paid her rent two days ago, Mrs. Ramirez, the landlady, who lived on the first floor, had mentioned nothing about losing a tenant. Kit had met the three stewardesses who occupied the large second-floor flat and the student nurse living on the third floor. She wondered which of them was moving.

Her silent question was instantly answered when two men came out carrying her garden-print sofa bed, followed by two others, each carrying a wicker rocker.

"Hey!" Kit shouted, running toward the truck. "What the devil are you doing with my furniture?"

An older man wearing a sweat-stained Stetson looked up from his clipboard. His twinkling blue eyes took in her shapely tanned legs, white cuffed shorts, blue sleeveless T-shirt, and tumble of fiery curls appreciatively. "Can I help you, miss?"

"You can tell me what you're doing with my furniture!" she repeated hotly.

"We're loading it in this truck." He grinned amicably.

She gave an exasperated sigh. "I can see that. On whose orders?"

"Rafe Morgan's."

48

"Is he upstairs?" she growled. At his affirmative nod, Kit thrust the partially eaten ice-cream cone and the laundry bag at him and ran past four gawking men into the building.

Upstairs, she stood in the petrified stillness of shock, dripping with perspiration and breathing heavily from taking the stairs two at a time. The first home she had made for herself, the first home she had ever been happy in was stripped to the bare white walls. She was so overcome, she missed the look of relief that crossed Rafe Morgan's face when he came out of the closet carrying a packing carton and saw her standing in the center of the room.

"What . . . how . . . why . . ." Kit was unable to form a coherent sentence. She stared at the aggressive picture he made in his rolled-sleeved tan workshirt and denims, a black Stetson pulled low on his forehead. She took a gulp of air, trying to steady herself, and closed her eyes, blocking out the vision of the man responsible for her naked apartment. Her resentment grew. The utter gall of this man taking away the only home she had ever really had!

Abruptly, her need to display some form of defiance faded. She realized the enormity of the situation she herself had precipitated. "I . . . I realize you must have been very upset," she managed at last, "but don't you think running me out of town is a little severe?"

Rafe gave a low chuckle, walked over, and placed his hands heavily on her shoulders. "I am not run-

49

ning you out of town. Just relocating you." He grinned.

She caught the devilish glint in the depths of his eyes, and her spirit was instantly revitalized. "Where to? Siberia?" she retorted sarcastically.

"No, my ranch."

Kit's eyes widened. "Why? I thought we agreed to end this as quickly as possible."

"I'm afraid it's a little too late for that now," he told her. Rafe walked over to the kitchen counter, picked up a folded newspaper, and slapped it into her hand.

Kit eyed the copy, raising a skeptical brow. "I fail to see what the new sewer project has to do with—"

"Not that," Rafe groaned, his mouth twitching with amusement. His long fingers flipped open the newspaper and pointed to a local column labeled *Spicy Bits*.

Kit's sarcastic attitude died a quick death. She silently read the gossip note. "It seems shipping and industrial magnate Rafe Morgan found love on the high seas with Texas newcomer Kit Forrester. We understand caterers are lining up for a real down-home engagement feast!"

She sank heavily onto the carpeted riser. "How could this have happened? Where did the papers get this story?" she asked anxiously, staring at the newspaper with unseeing eyes.

Rafe shrugged his broad shoulders and strolled over to look out the tiny dormer window. "You'd be surprised how fast this type of news travels. A man in my position is fair game for all sorts of gossip."

"I am so sorry," she said in a low whisper, her nerveless fingers letting the paper fall to the floor. "Honestly, Rafe, I never meant to have this happen." Kit was silent for a long moment; then she took a deep breath. "I'll go to the newspapers and tell them the truth. They can print a retraction. I'll tell Mr. Shippley and make sure his daughters know, too," she told him dully, completely humiliated by this ghastly turn of events. In all her adolescent escapades she had never involved anyone else. She had been verbally disruptive at home and school; she had destroyed property of marginal value in a variety of pranks; and she had been a discipline problem. But she had never set out to deliberately hurt another person.

"Do you think anyone would believe you?" Rafe asked bluntly. "That's why I'm getting you out of here and taking you to my ranch. I want control over this situation."

"That doesn't make any sense," she said, completely puzzled by his actions. "Wouldn't it be better to let this whole thing die a natural death?" She got up and walked over to him.

"Aren't you forgetting who your new employer is?" he reminded her evenly. "That story is bound to get around, too."

"I'll get another job. I'll even leave the city," she told him quickly. "Don't you realize that if we're seen together, it's only going to cause more talk? For heaven's sake, if I'm living at your ranch, everyone will think—" She stopped, remembering something Marybeth Shippley had said. Kit reached out and grabbed Rafe's shoulders roughly, forcing him to look at her. "Now I understand," she breathed sharply, her eyes narrowing dangerously into twin blue-white chips. "You're doing this to spite Tracy Shippley! You're going to use me to make her jealous, aren't you? You're going to get even with her for refusing to go on that cruise with you."

Rafe turned his broad back on her, shrugging his shoulders, not saying a word to refute her statements.

"I can't believe it!" Kit fumed, pacing the floor with short, angry strides. "That's what you want, isn't it? To punish Tracy so she'll come crawling back. To turn her into some submissive, subservient woman who jumps at your every command."

"I'll make it worth your while."

"Make it worth my while!" Her jaw dropped. "Oh . . . you make me so mad!" she exploded, slamming her hand against the kitchen counter. "No. I refuse." Kit's voice was firm, her emotions under complete control. "You can just tell your men to unload that truck and put my house back in order," she directed and crossed her arms over her breasts in complete self-confidence.

Rafe's hands curved roughly over her bare upper arms and snapped her poise. "And who is going to

52

put my house in order?" he asked coldly, his firm lips twisting into a cruel sneer. "If you think you can waltz away from this tangled web *you* created, think again, sweetheart. I can make sure you never work in this state or in any decent job. I want you and everything you own right under my thumb." He gave her a hard shake, then released her and turned back to the window.

Kit blinked rapidly. A shiver of pure fright snaked down her spine at the memory of Rafe's granite hard features. This time the tables were turned. The spider was in danger of being devoured by the captive fly. Wearily, she rubbed her face, exhaling in frustration. "How long will this charade have to last?"

A slow, triumphant smile spread over Rafe's face as he studied the tips of his boots. It was quickly replaced by an impassive expression before he turned back to Kit. "Two or three weeks at the most. Tracy is still in New York, but I'm sure Marybeth will call her about the news item."

A knock on the apartment door prevented Kit's reply.

"We're all packed, boss," said the man with the Stetson whom Kit had seen earlier. "Anything left up here?"

Rafe indicated the packing box on the floor. "Do you have anything else?" he asked her.

"Just my bike. It's the red one in the garage out back," she replied dully.

The man nodded and left.

"No car?" Rafe inquired, watching her dejected manner with enigmatic eyes.

Kit shook her head. "After numerous transplants, it committed suicide six months ago," she told him ruefully. "San Antonio's bus system sure beats gas and insurance prices."

He laughed, sliding an arm around her shoulders. "Shall we head for home?"

"Let me get the rest of my personal things," she muttered hastily, shrugging out from under a most proprietary arm.

"They're already packed."

"I really would have preferred to do it myself," Kit returned stiffly. "I don't like strangers going through my things."

"I packed them myself," he announced, holding the door open.

"Oh, that makes all the difference in the world," she retorted with heavy sarcasm. Kit paused and turned back to look at her empty penthouse garret. Like General MacArthur, she would return.

Once outside, Kit lowered herself into a sleek black Porsche bearing the license plate MORGAN-2. "How far out of town is your ranch?" she queried, wiggling comfortably in the white leather bucket seat. She was surprised by the leg room and opulence the sports car afforded.

"It's eighty miles northwest of the city," Rafe told her, stopping for a traffic signal by the 750-foot

Tower of the Americas, which stood as emphatic as an exclamation point in the heart of San Antonio.

"Is it very big?"

"Big enough," he said, shifting gears and sending the powerful car surging forward. "How did you happen to settle in Texas after leaving Long Island?"

Kit shivered against his probing and knew it had nothing to do with the car's air conditioning. "How do you know I'm from New York?"

"It's your accent," he told her with a smile. "I also did a little checking."

"Looking for a pedigree?" she countered acidly, a hard knot twisting in her stomach.

His right hand left the steering wheel to squeeze her bare thigh. "Why don't you tell me a little about yourself, just in case I'm asked any questions about my fiancée."

Kit picked up his hand and firmly replaced it on the wheel. Resentment was growing inside her. She didn't like Rafe Morgan's masterful domination. She didn't like being manipulated and she didn't like not being in control. She wondered just how much he knew about her. Logically, he would have had time to read only her employee records from Shippley Electronics.

She chewed her thumbnail reflectively. He already knew she was a liar. Maybe once he found out just how troublesome and undesirable she was, he would think twice about wanting her to pose as his fiancée. He'd probably turn the car around and bring her back home. He'd end the charade, Kit concluded, brightening considerably. The truth shall set you free; well, maybe not the *whole* truth.

"If you're expecting to hear about the happy, all-American family in the proverbial rose-covered cottage, forget it. My parents were permanent residents of the state of intoxication. One New Year's Eve they got a little careless and on September thirteenth, Black Friday as my mother often called it, I arrived. One of those little household accidents you hear so much about."

"Aren't you being unnecessarily—"

Kit's cold, harsh laugh interrupted him. Her eyes focused on the swiftly passing cypress and pecan trees. "My parents wanted a perpetual good time. I interrupted that. They pushed me on my maternal grandmother, who was not thrilled with raising a child at her advanced age. Grandma expected a petite, dainty little girl she could dress in lace and ruffles, someone who played with dolls and tea sets and was perfectly behaved. Instead, she got a tree-climbing, obstinate tomboy who just grew and grew. When she died, I went back home. My folks got a divorce. My mother got custody of the gin, my father got the Scotch. A series of strict boarding schools tried to whip me into shape. You can see how well they did," Kit added with false gaiety. She clamped her mouth shut, instantly regretting her confession. She had always smiled and showed her surface self to others, keeping back the private person with the hurting memories, never sharing large parts of her life with anyone.

"How did you end up in Texas?"

"About fourteen months ago a friend of mine was coming to join her husband at Lackland Air Force Base. My job was going to be replaced by a computer, so I decided to come with her. Luckily, my car stayed healthy enough to make the long trip. I found a job at Shippley. I've been taking a few night courses toward a college degree, and—"

"Went on a cruise," Rafe finished with an amused drawl.

"Ah, yes, the cruise," Kit repeated with heavy irony. Her eyes were making an intense study of the other cars on the heavily congested highway. "That certainly changed my life," she muttered. "Are there any other Morgans running around at your ranch?" she asked sweetly, wanting to change the direction of the conversation.

"There usually are this time of year," Rafe told her, nosing the Porsche into the high-speed lane. "But my parents, my older sister and her husband and two daughters are visiting relatives in Spain until the end of August."

"And they all live with you?" Kit questioned in astonishment.

"No," he laughed. "My folks live year-round in Acapulco and my sister's family lives in Dallas. I'm taking care of my nephew, Matt Bishop, while they're in Europe."

57

"That's the boy in your wallet photo," Kit said, recalling the tow-headed youngster who looked to be about eight years old.

"That's Matt," Rafe concurred. "He's been giving his folks a bit of a problem. You can help me keep an eye on him."

"From secretary to baby-sitter," she muttered wryly.

"You don't like kids?" Rafe asked almost brusquely, taking his eyes off the traffic to glance at her.

"I happen to love kids. I've spent the better part of my life being an obnoxious child," she returned brightly. "This just takes a bit of adjusting."

"I have the distinct feeling Matt isn't the only handful I'm going to have to contend with" was his dry rejoinder.

"Between the two of us," Kit said and smiled evilly, "you may get more than you bargained for." She reached over and gave *his* knee a firm, warning squeeze.

A bit of elegance amid the simplicity of the Old West, Kit thought lyrically when the Porsche turned through an ornate wrought-iron arch that marked the Morgan ranch. It took another quarter mile before a sprawling Spanish hacienda with a red-tiled roof came into view.

Rafe slid the sports car between a jeep and a flatbed paneled truck, respectfully marked MOR-

GAN-3 and MORGAN-4, at the far end of the ranch's main house near the stables.

"You'll have the guest cottage," he told Kit as they exited from the car. "The moving van will be here shortly. In the meantime, I'll show you around."

"It's very beautiful," Kit said sincerely, taking in the magnificent view of house, towering trees, and the vast stretch of fertile land beyond. "It looks new," she stated in surprise.

"It is. I've only lived here for the last two years, myself," he returned amiably, his hand settling familiarly in the curve of her waist and guiding her toward the house.

Kit frowned thoughtfully, looking at the tall enigmatic man beside her. "For some reason I got the distinct impression that you were one of the founding pillars of the city's society."

"No, ma'am," he drawled, giving her another one of his potent, wide, dimpled grins. "You have to be at least two generations beyond rustlers and robber barons to attain that status. This all came about from a little scrap of land I won in a navy poker game. The damn thing just kept oozing oil."

Their shared laughter was interrupted by a high-pitched whine followed by a sharp yip coming from the barn. A small yowling bundle of silver fur charged out, almost knocking Kit off her feet.

"This," Rafe said disgustedly, steadying her and giving a sharp command to the dog, "is Nosey."

Kit eyed the well-groomed schnauzer with considerable amusement. The dog was trying to carry out the command of sit, but his body was vibrating with excitement over a visitor. She got down on her haunches, snapped her fingers, and was immediately assaulted by the rambunctious, furry bundle. "He's not a cattle dog," she said, grinning up at Rafe.

"That's an understatement," he replied. "My mother rescued him from the animal shelter and is trying to find a home for him."

"Why all the bandages?" she inquired, indicating the wrapped stub of a tail and one covered, uncropped ear.

"He made the unfortunate mistake of annoying a barn cat with a new litter and one of the horses."

"I see his name is most appropriate," Kit chuckled, giving Nosey a final pat.

The cool interior of the main house was stunning in its spaciousness and decor. The entry foyer was as large as Kit's entire apartment, with a terrazzo-tiled floor and white stucco walls that gleamed in the sun from the skylight. On her left was a massive living room with an arched fireplace. Intricately carved doors led into a huge banquet-sized dining room. Both were elegant in a mixture of Mediterranean furnishings, Oriental carpets, and a few carefully chosen paintings.

The family room with its beamed ceiling and full-wall stone fireplace seemed to be the center of the house. Here the colors of the Southwest dominated

—warm tones of beige, white, and brown. A comfortable modular seating unit was the focal point of the room. A white shag rug covered the plank-style floor, an entertainment unit balanced the wall opposite the fireplace, and Apache wall hangings and stunning desert paintings finished the overall effect.

There was a rugged individualism about the room that reflected the man who owned the ranch. Kit mentally added a few green plants, flowered accent pillows—pure feminine touches that would soften the masculine lines and make the room a shared haven for two. Her mind skidded to an abrupt halt. It wouldn't be her in this house, but Tracy Shippley; once her performance was finished she would be out of Rafe Morgan's life.

His voice cut through her musings. "There's a kitchen through there and six bedrooms and four baths upstairs."

"You have a very beautiful home," Kit told him with obvious sincerity, and for some odd reason she felt he was pleased with her admission.

A delicate cough from the service hall caused them both to turn and find a small, wiry woman watching them with keen interest in her dark eyes.

Rafe smiled indulgently. "Teresa Lopez, this is Kit Forrester."

Kit didn't miss the older woman's raised eyebrows at her casual attire, and suddenly she wished the shorts and T-shirt would magically transform themselves into a demure outfit with a high neckline and long skirt. Instead, she took a deep breath, gave Teresa her most gracious smile, and extended her hand.

"Teresa really runs this place," Rafe said with a smile. "Has Matt come back yet?"

Teresa shook her head. "I placed some refreshments out on the patio for you both," she told them in a lightly accented voice. "If you need anything, senorita, please just let me know."

"Thank you." Kit smiled warmly and was pleased by the friendly light in the older woman's velvety dark eyes.

"I didn't get a chance to tell Matt I was moving you into the guest house," Rafe explained, leading Kit through the sliding glass doors into a large screened porch. "He left at the crack of dawn to help some of the hands bring a few horses down."

Kit nodded mutely, accepting a tall, fruit-filled glass of sangría he had poured. Her eyes scanned the ornate terrace and barbecue area to settle on the glittering waters of a fabulous in-ground pool shimmering in the distance.

"That's your cottage, just beyond the pool," Rafe told her. A truck horn interrupted any further conversation. "There's the van. You sit and relax while I help them settle everything into the cottage."

She watched his tall, rugged figure cross the terrace. She put the glass of wine down, pushed herself out of the thickly padded wrought-iron patio chair, and stared at the screen door. The porch felt like a cage. Kit's fingers closed around the door handle and pushed the door open, letting her feet take her into the back courtyard. The garden was filled with a collection of flowering cactus and succulent plants as well as the more traditional variety.

Kit followed the laughter and lilting Spanish conversation drifting from the side of the house and found a produce truck being unloaded. Teresa was carefully inspecting each basket of vegetables and fruit. Jamming her hands into the patch pockets of her brief white shorts, Kit silently pondered her predicament. There was one inherent danger in continuing this masquerade: Rafe Morgan. He had a potent, virile charm and a laid-back personality that she was finding impossible to ignore. The longer she stayed and the more deeply involved she got, the harder it was going to be when it came time to leave.

A low wolf whistle caused her to look up just as she entered the pool area. It came from a young man clad in black swim trunks who had just emerged from one of the striped cabanas.

Kit stood watching him walk toward her, his boyish features coming into clearer focus with each step. The sandy, sun-streaked hair was a little too shaggy; his slender, long-limbed frame had yet to broaden; his height matched her own.

"Well, well, well," he drawled, his brown eyes frankly appraising her full, curving figure. "Don't tell me you stowed away on that delivery truck just to meet my uncle?"

Kit's eyes widened in surprise. This must be Rafe's nephew, Matt Bishop, who appeared to be ten years older than the kid in the photograph she had seen in his uncle's wallet.

He chuckled, mistaking her silence for confirmation. "I hate to burst your bubble, honey, but Uncle Rafe's already engaged." He put a hand on either side of the pool fence, effectively blocking her escape. "You might do better to look in my direction. I understand you older women are always grateful for the attentions of a younger man. I could show you a real good time."

"Really?" The most audacious glint lit her wide, unmistakably beautiful blue eyes. Instead of stammering and blushing like a gauche schoolgirl, Kit focused her gaze with unwavering scrutiny on his youthful face.

Matt's brow puckered and he swallowed convulsively, his body fidgeting in acute discomfort.

She smiled and removed his hands. "Your first mistake was reminding me that I was *older* than you," she intoned dryly. "If you're trying to perfect a line, never use the word *grateful,* and—"

Rafe's voice interrupted her. "You just get back, Matt?" he asked, giving his young nephew a companionable slap on the back.

Matt nodded slowly, looking from his uncle to the tall redhead.

"I take it you two have met?" Rafe inquired, eyeing the quiet pair with interest.

"Matt introduced himself," Kit returned pleasantly, "but I'm afraid I didn't get the opportunity."

Rafe fingered his thick dark mustache, more than slightly perplexed. He then performed the necessary introductions. "I've moved Kit into the guest cottage," he told Matt, sliding an arm around her shoulders. "I'll show you your new home while my suddenly shy nephew finishes his swim."

The guest cottage was an elegant miniature of the main house. The large living room was decorated in a monochromatic scheme of blues, which were carried into the small dining-kitchen area and the two bedrooms. The bathroom caught Kit's eye immediately. It was an old-fashioned affair with a pedestal sink and a high, claw-footed antique tub with a whirlpool attachment. There had been only a shower in her tiny apartment, and the thought of relaxing in chin-high, frothing water was a luxury—one Kit knew she didn't deserve.

She had done something to ruin a man's life. It seemed wrong that she should receive such royal treatment. She was here to serve a penance, not enjoy heavenly opulence.

"You're suddenly very quiet." Rafe's deep voice invaded her self-reflection.

She turned back to find him watching her. Kit shrugged, lowering her somber eyes from his compelling gaze. "It's all very beautiful. I guess I've said that at least three times. This is far better than I deserve after getting you in this situation." Her voice was low, uncharacteristically sober and contrite as she studied the pale blue carpet.

"If you're trying to talk yourself out of here—" His voice was hard and warning, his hands like steel clamps gripping the soft skin of her upper arms.

She shook her head. "I told you I'd play my part. I don't go back on my word," Kit retorted defensively, trying to shrug out of his grip. Her efforts proved futile.

Rafe's hands slid over her shoulders, pulling her roughly against the full length of his body. His hard tongue deliberately parted her soft mouth, lustily savoring its moist delights. One large hand held the nape of her neck; the other settled at the base of her spine, pressing her intimately against him.

Kit's heart throbbed in a frantic crescendo against her crushed breasts. An unaccustomed burst of heat seared every nerve in her body. Her hands pushed weakly against his shoulders and she finally managed to recapture her breath from his demanding mouth.

"You're going to have to get used to that if we're going to appear the convincing engaged couple," Rafe murmured huskily against her ear.

Kit swallowed unsteadily, pulling herself free from his embrace. "Somehow I don't think you need any extra practice," she parried sarcastically, trying to control her own tumultuous feelings.

The intercom buzzed and Rafe picked up the telephone. He spoke quietly, then replaced the receiver. "I've got a business call at the house."

"Go ahead." Kit waved a carefree hand toward the door. "I'll finish putting my things away."

Rafe opened the back door and Nosey bounded in with a joyous bark, punching Kit with his front paws in a boisterous welcome. She calmed him down with a few pats, then with the schnauzer literally under her feet, wandered into the larger bedroom and began transferring her clothes from the packing boxes into an elegant Mediterranean-style dresser. Her few items of furniture had been neatly stored in the smaller bedroom, and she found the movers had even packed the contents of her kitchen cabinets and refrigerator. Kit had just finished pouring herself a soda and feeding a cracker to Nosey when a sharp rap sounded on the front door. She opened it to find a denim-clad Matt Bishop nervously fingering the collar of his tan knit shirt.

"Hello." Kit looked at him, then smiled. "Come in and have a drink."

Matt shook his head. "I heard Uncle Rafe on the phone back at the house." He rubbed his neck restlessly as he trailed after her into the living room. "Did you tell him?" he asked urgently.

"What did you expect me to tell him? That you propositioned me?"

"How much is it going to cost me?"

"Your firstborn child," Kit quipped sarcastically, thinking these people certainly relied on money to handle their problems.

He looked up from an intense study of his boots and stared at her oddly. "What do you want?"

"Not a damn thing," Kit said matter-of-factly, reseating herself on the patterned sofa. "After all, you were only joking." She studied his face, groaning when his cheeks suffused with color. "Oh, my, you really meant it!"

"Look," Matt stammered, dropping into the cushion next to her, "I thought you were just another gate-crasher. Ever since that article on Uncle Rafe appeared in the local business magazine, he's had nothing but interested females turning up at the ranch, the club, and his office."

Kit scratched her cheek reflectively. Now she understood why Rafe had been skeptical about believing her story of inventing him as her fictitious ship partner. "I didn't see the magazine article, but I sympathize with your problem. It seems you've become the latest fad." She smiled gently. "I assumed you were trying to scare me off."

"I guess I was half hoping you'd take me up on my proposition," Matt admitted lamely, averting his brown eyes.

"Ah, yes, your older woman theory." She deliberated thoughtfully. "I would think you'd get enough action from high school girls."

"Yeah, well. I kind of have a tough time and I figured you'd be a little more experienced and . . ." His voice trailed off miserably.

Kit cleared her throat, feeling her cheeks turn as

crimson as her companion's. "Despite my advanced age, my strict parochial upbringing has been very hard to shed. You've probably got more experience than I have."

"I don't really have any," Matt admitted sheepishly.

That makes two of us, she thought ruefully. Kit reached out and patted his shoulder in silent understanding. "Don't worry about it. At seventeen you've still got time to perfect a line that will dazzle the girls." She took a long swallow of cola, watching with satisfaction as her young companion relaxed. She decided to shift the conversation to less personal lines. "I hope you've got a horse that won't clash with my hair and that's big enough to keep my feet from dragging in the dust."

"We've got a whole stableful. Are you a good rider?"

"The first thing I did when I arrived in Texas was take riding lessons. The man in charge said I was a natural," she informed Matt with a captivating smile.

"I didn't see any riding gear with your things," interposed Rafe's voice from the back kitchen door, causing both Kit and Matt to jump guiltily.

"I make do with what I have," she informed him lightly, trying to read the enigmatic expression on his face. Just how much of their conversation had he overheard?

His casual manner and good-natured grin seemed

to allay her fears. "I came to tell you that dinner will be ready in an hour and to see if you need anything."

Kit shook her head. "Well, if that's the case," she announced perkily, looking from grinning nephew to grinning uncle and smiling herself, "I think I'll toss both of you gentlemen out of here so I can try out that marvelous bathtub."

An hour and fifteen minutes later a slightly frazzled Kit answered the knock on the back door. It was Rafe looking extremely handsome in a double-breasted blue blazer over an open-necked white silk shirt and slacks.

"I see that, like the rest of the fairer sex, you have the habit of running late," he said in his teasing drawl. His tall body leaned negligently against the door frame. "Although I must admit it was worth the wait," he added, frankly assessing the softly defined curves of her body under the off-white Chinese-style dress with red piping trim and cap sleeves.

In all her life Kit had never received so many compliments or been made to feel so special and valuable with just a look. Of course, her conscience warned, Rafe was perfecting his role of dutiful fiancé. She adopted her best blasé attitude, giving her side-parted copper hair an unnecessary fluffing. "I'm afraid I had a furry little helper who contributed to my tardiness," she smiled sweetly, gesturing toward Nosey. The dog was sitting at a distinct tilt in the center of the room, his panting, pink tongue giving a comical expression to his boxy face. "You mentioned his curiosity but forgot to tell me he was also a thief."

"What did he steal?"

"He seems to have a penchant for ladies' lingerie and for getting tangled in pantyhose," she elaborated in an accusing tone that brought a chuckle from the dog's master.

"That's just part of his charm," Rafe said with a grin, sliding an arm around her waist and gently heading her toward the patio.

Teresa had decorated the round table with a shimmering centerpiece of floating candles and colorful magnolia blossoms on a pristine white cloth with flowered napkins. It was an intimate, yet informal meal with a delicious almond chicken casserole over wild rice for an entrée. Kit was pleased with the way the conversation flowed during the meal. She was able to learn more about the cattle and horse breeding done on the ranch and joined Rafe and Matt in a lively discussion on current events.

Garnering a promise of a predawn ride with Kit, Matt excused himself after dessert and disappeared into the game room, while Rafe secured two after-dinner liqueurs. Kit wandered out to the pool area to watch the late evening sunset. When she woke this morning, she had never expected to end her day anyplace other than her own attic apartment. Now she was a resident, albeit a temporary one, in a wholly new environment. There was a touch of fantasy about the day. The only reality was the silver schnauzer who kept nudging her leg for tasty tidbits during dinner and now padded along at her side.

Kit settled in a cushioned deck chair and was absently rubbing Nosey's ears when Rafe returned. She accepted the snifter of brandy with a polite thank you before hesitatingly introducing a topic she was positive would draw his angry response.

"I don't want to put a damper on the end of a very lovely evening," Kit said slowly, then at Rafe's arched brow, quickly continued. "It's just that . . . you don't know when Tracy is going to be returning, so our little charade may not be starting for a week and I . . . well, I'm just not used to sitting around all day. I've had some type of job since I was sixteen. Frankly, the sybaritic life of luxury and do-nothing will drive me crazy. Can you understand that?" She looked at him appealingly with her wide blue eyes.

He studied her sweetly rounded face in the dusky light and for just a moment looked as if he were going to say something. Rafe gave a sharp shake to clear his head. He set his glass down, pushed himself out of his chair, and stood before her, feet planted firmly apart, hands in his trouser pockets. "What would you suggest?"

She suddenly felt dwarfed by the aggressively male picture he made and coughed nervously. "Let me go back to my job. I'd—"

"No," he said sharply. "I'm not taking any

chances of having you run out and leave me in a most embarrassing position."

"I told you before I wouldn't do that," Kit rallied spiritedly, setting her own glass on the table. She lunged to her feet, putting her hands on her hips in a defiant gesture that rivaled his. Even with her high heels Rafe still topped her height by a few inches. "If I sit around here and eat Teresa's cooking all day with nothing to do but swim and take an occasional horseback ride, you're going to come home to a fat, prunelike creature with saddle sores!" she snapped belligerently, stamping her foot angrily on the concrete.

A slow grin broke across Rafe's granite-hard features. "All right, honey, how about if I give you a little project to work on?" he countered silkily.

"What kind of little project?" Kit asked suspiciously, not trusting the light in his brown eyes.

"Follow me, sweetheart," he drawled, grabbing her arm and all but pulling her into the house.

Kit finally managed to pry herself loose from his steellike grip when he flipped on the light switch in his den. The thick gold carpeting and light drapes, along with a small grouping of Indian carvings, balanced the room's paneled, book-lined walls and massive oak desk.

Rafe pulled a manila folder from the basket on top of the desk, motioning Kit over for a better view of his mysterious project.

"I've gotten together with a small group of close

friends on a very special proposal. It's an accident and burn treatment center that we're building in San Antonio," he told her proudly, pointing to a small architectural drawing of the proposed clinic. "This is a personal project, totally unrelated to my business dealings, although I've got a few key men handling land acquisitions and construction bids."

"How could I help?" Kit asked.

"My secretary has been doing most of the correspondence, but she's really got more than she can handle at the office," he told her, relaxing in his black executive chair. "What I'd like you to do is familiarize yourself with the file, see where everything is at this early stage, and coordinate all the latest developments." He paused, watching her settle on the corner of the big desk and leaf through the large stack of material. "There are plenty of letters to write. We need equipment and supply estimates. Contribution letters need to be written with a personal touch. I know I can trust you to handle everything."

Kit looked from the folder to the man in the chair, instantly liking this side of Rafe Morgan. "I'd love to do it," she answered without hesitation. "I promise I'll do the best job possible."

"I never doubted that," he returned with a smile. Suddenly he reached up and pulled her head down, planting a hard kiss on her soft mouth. "Just to seal the deal."

CHAPTER FOUR

Kit held her breath with wonder. The rising sun had etched the morning clouds in silver and streaked the sky in coral. Slowly nature dipped her paintbrush into a colorful palette and turned the sleeping gray landscape into an artistic triumph, rich in depth and striking in contrast.

As Kit turned her smiling face toward Matt Bishop, the leather saddle creaked under her shifting weight. "It's incredible," she laughed delightedly, eagerly refocusing on the wondrous scene. The sprawling Morgan hacienda with its overhanging red-tiled roof and long balconies lay in the fertile valley below. Rolling green pasturelands, heavily dotted with grazing brown and white Brangus cattle and magnificent horses, stretched out before her for what seemed an eternity.

Matt had brought her to a high grassy knoll slightly over a mile from the ranch to enjoy the sunrise. He had kept up a running commentary on the various flora and fauna, interspersed with seemingly casual questions that required her response.

Kit sensed that Matt needed someone other than family to talk to. She remembered how confused and turbulent her own youth had been for lack of available confidants. She answered all his questions directly and honestly, volunteering neither advice nor criticism. A companionable alliance was forming and solidifying between them.

Zodiac, Rafe's black saddle-bred stallion, tossed his massive head, snorting his discontent at remaining stationary for so long. Kit soothingly patted his glossy, powerful neck, casting a teasing sidelong glance at Matt. "Do you think that wide-heeled, pigeon-toed Appaloosa of yours can handle a race?" she asked, her blue eyes wide with affected innocence.

Matt flashed her a toothy grin, edging the gray shaded and spotted gelding alongside the stallion. "Thor and I will give you a run for your money, Kit," he drawled easily, and pulling his dusty brown Stetson low to shade his eyes, he gave a loud yelp.

A hurricane of thundering hooves pelted the ground, crushing milkweeds and pin flowers and sending prairie dogs and ground squirrels scuttling into their holes for protection.

Kit felt alive and free on the back of the big black stallion. She moved in unison with the horse, her body low and flexible, her weight evenly distributed through thighs, knees, and feet. Invisible currents of electricity energized her soul. She urged Zodiac into a faster gallop, his flowing black mane and her copper hair blowing like pennants in the wind.

Approaching the stables, both riders pulled their horses into a sedate cantor, with Matt laughingly conceding her victory. Kit spied Rafe's tall figure holding the corral gate open for them. She had felt unaccountably disappointed when he had failed to join them this morning, severely scolding herself for even noticing his absence.

"One of the most natural seats on a horse I've ever seen," she heard Matt tell his uncle.

"That's just one of her many attributes I noticed right off" was Rafe's teasing rejoinder.

Kit dismounted in one fluid movement, then led Zodiac toward the gate, her cheeks warming under Rafe's compelling gaze. He looked more dominant than ever, his muscular physique accented by an impeccably tailored beige business suit. Uncomfortably aware of her own dishevelment and worn clothing, Kit pushed nervous fingers through her tangled hair, a weak smile pasted on her lips.

She was totally unaware of the arresting picture she made, her tall, curving figure in slim jeans and a green plaid shirt. Her complexion glowed from the energy of the ride, and the fiery copper hair curled riotously from heat and perspiration.

Zodiac came snuffling and scenting until the feelers of his muzzle tickled the back of her neck. Reluctantly she handed the reins to Matt, giving the horse a farewell pat.

"Looks like you made a conquest," Rafe acknowledged with lazy amusement.

"More than likely it's the scent of my oatmeal face soap," she returned lightly. Kit deliberately focused her eyes on the pitted gateposts rather than on the dangerously attractive man at her side.

"Don't you believe it," Matt interjected. "She's fantastic with horses. She even warmed Zodiac's bit in her hands this morning," he reported before leading the lathered animals for a cool-down walk.

"I stand corrected," Rafe remarked thoughtfully. "It seems you made two conquests this morning." He casually draped a sinewy arm across her shoulders.

Kit shrugged, trying to dislodge his arm. "We had time to get better acquainted on our ride." She stole a quick glance at his profile. "I suppose you're used to the gorgeous sunrises out here," she commented idly.

His thumb and forefinger slowly massaged his dark mustache. "Ordinarily I would have joined you," he answered slowly, watching the ease with which Kit matched his long, leisurely strides, "but I had a lot on my mind last night and I'm afraid I overslept."

Kit raised a burnished brow. So he had spent a restless night; he was probably having second thoughts. She stopped walking and turned toward him, seizing what she thought was a golden opportunity. "Listen, if you want to call it quits and end this charade, just say so. I can be packed and out of here in under an hour, out of town by tomorrow." She took a deep breath and looked him straight in the eye. "We've got a built-in audience out here." She nodded toward three ranch hands unloading feed sacks near the barn. "We can have one hell of a fight. Yell at me, hit me, then you can say good riddance to bad rubbish and—"

Rafe's mouth, hard and commanding, fastened on her mobile lips, stealing her breath away and swallowing her words.

"You weren't supposed to do *that,*" Kit groaned, pushing against his broad chest, her shoulders slumping dejectedly.

He chuckled softly, his fingers gripping her chin, forcing her face up for his inspection. "It was quicker than waiting for your battery to run down." His brown eyes studied her luminous, upturned features; his good-natured grin turned into an angry scowl. "What makes you think I'd ever slap you?" Rafe growled fiercely. "And I don't like you calling yourself rubbish, either. You seem to have an annoying habit of deprecating yourself at every turn."

79

"It comes from years of institutional living," Kit returned coolly, lowering her eyes to study the silken weave in his bronze and beige necktie. "I'm under no illusions about myself. I've never been one to collect compliments and lovers; only strict, impersonal discipline."

"So you built this wall around yourself, convinced you're unlovable and worthless."

She pulled loose from his strong grip, tossing her head carelessly. His words had touched a raw nerve, but over the years she had schooled herself to remain uncaring and aloof. "I suppose I could have gone the other way, indiscriminately seeking affection from a variety of men and reaping not only love but monetary rewards as well."

"But *you* didn't," he stated emphatically, his dark eyes narrowing at her suggestion.

"Amazon prostitutes are at a distinct disadvantage," she returned dryly. "Men like to be the dominant ones."

"You're a great little philosopher, aren't you, Kit?"

"Well," she drawled nastily, her fingers sliding up to tighten the perfectly proportioned knot of his necktie, "isn't that what I'm here for? You're trying to dominate Tracy Shippley."

Rafe's hand came up, capturing her fingers, holding them tightly against his chest. One dark brow rose speculatively. "You think you know me so well." His words sounded like a warning, but a devilish grin broke the serious expression on his tanned face, and the dimples in his cheeks deepened attractively. "But that's what engagements are for, Kit. To let each partner find out more about the other." His voice flowed like treacle after her venomous barb. "It's going to be most enjoyable taming you. Those schools did little to break your fiery spirit."

Kit twisted her hands free, her eyes glittering an icy alert. "Unlike your horses, I can't be broken. I warned you about that before."

"Maybe I can bend you a little," he returned easily, his hand settling on top of her burnished hair. Rafe frowned when he felt the heat radiating from her uncovered head. "You should have worn your hat," he admonished sharply. He bent down, grasped her shin, and examined her foot as if she were a mare in need of a blacksmith. "Where are your riding boots?"

"Don't own either," Kit said blithely, stamping her doeskin-shod foot on the hard earth. "The Indians rode for years in moccasins."

Rafe grunted. "You're going to catch one hell of a sunburn without a hat," he warned, letting his hand settle at the small of her back as he guided her toward the garages.

"The sun's not that powerful early in the morning, and I'll be working inside during the day," she reminded him.

"I left a few more notes in the study for you, along with the names and phone numbers of everyone you'll be working with. I'll let them know you're coordinating the project and to send you detailed reports."

"Fine." Kit eyed the fleet of cars with interest. The Mercedes and Porsche shared consecutively numbered license plates with two pickup trucks, a station wagon, and a jeep. "You don't own an auto dealership by some remote chance, do you?" she asked sweetly.

"Nope," he said and grinned, "just an insurance company."

"How clever of you to diversify," she intoned dryly, watching him slide into the low-slung sports car with considerable grace for a man of his size.

"Kit?" His call was a whisper, and she was forced to lower her head, her face centered in the car's open window. "Since you so carefully noted our audience," Rafe commented silkily, imprisoning her face between his large hands, "it seems most appropriate to give my fiancée a good-bye kiss."

His mouth stole her breath away and robbed her of poise. The touch of his firm lips sent warm vibrations coursing down her spine. Her lashes fluttered open and she stared into his lambent brown eyes. It was impossible to ignore their silent message. She pulled away, her cheeks burning with color that did not come from the heat of the sun.

Eyeing her with an audacious glint, Rafe gunned the engine to life. "I'll call you later," he told her with a wide grin before sending the sports car down the drive.

Kit expelled a long-held breath. She was blatantly aware of how easily he was able to arouse her. That had never happened to her before. She was going to have to take some drastic steps to control her emotions. Maybe if she recited the multiplication tables . . .

Kit tidied the guest cottage, showered, and changed into a pair of tan cotton slacks and a rust and beige sleeveless print blouse. She had intended to have a quick cup of coffee, but Teresa wasn't letting her out of the cheery yellow and green kitchen until she did justice to a breakfast that would have fed a family of four.

Groaning, Kit put her hand over her plate, vigorously shaking her head to refuse a third pancake and a second fried egg. She immediately decided a compromise over meals was needed or she'd end up as wide as she was tall!

Over a companionable cup of coffee, Teresa reluctantly agreed to feed her a light breakfast and lunch and drop the senorita before her name. Kit, in turn, promised to do justice to the dinners. She was surprised when Teresa told her Rafe expected her to help plan the weekly menus. She had always wanted to improve her cooking skills and shyly inquired if Teresa would mind if she helped with dinner. She was rewarded with a smile from the velvet-eyed housekeeper.

Promptly at nine, Kit was comfortably settled in Rafe's study excitedly attacking her new job. She spent the next few hours assimilating and organizing the file information and arranging a handy index system. Construction bids on the proposed architectural design had been submitted by various groups and awarded to the Stanford Development Corporation. Ground breaking on the burn treatment center would begin once the papers had been finalized on the land acquisition. According to the file memos, the legalities should be completed within two weeks.

The large parcel of vacant land, in one of San Antonio's prime areas, was being donated by K.C. Whittier. Although Kit had never met Whittier, she did know his assistant, Phyllis Vogel. They had worked on the publicity committee for the secretaries' club. She knew from Phyllis that her boss was somewhat eccentric and spent little time in his office. K.C., whose wealth derived from gold prospecting during the twenties, still enjoyed heading back to nature via deep-sea fishing, archaeological digs, and wildlife trips.

Kit's next step was composing letters to hospital equipment and supply companies for cost estimates on furnishing the clinic with the most modern medical tools available. She was working on her second rough draft when Matt poked his head into the den to announce lunch.

"I haven't finished digesting breakfast yet," she said, grinning ruefully, snapping off the electric typewriter, and flexing her cramped fingers. "What have you been up to all morning?" she inquired, pointedly eyeing his damp, mud-stained clothes.

"I've been grooming the horses we just sold. They're being shipped out today," Matt explained easily. "I see you're settling right into work."

"It's very interesting, too," Kit told him, reclining against the rich brown leather chair. "I'm composing some bid letters for hospital equipment."

"I thought I'd go into town later, maybe even get a haircut," Matt said hesitantly. "What do you think?"

"About your going into town or the haircut?" she teased, her blue eyes smiling at his thoughtful expression.

"Aw, come on, Kit." He shuffled into the room, draping his loose-jointed body into a gold leather chair. The musical tones of the doorbell echoed through the house. "That's probably the mail. Uncle Rafe told me to have you go through it and he'd call you later."

Kit gnawed her lower lip pensively. She was becoming more involved with Rafe Morgan's business and life than she had anticipated. But to be truthful, it was not unpleasant. It would, however, make it that much harder on her when her role of fiancée ended and it came time to leave. Well, she decided stoically, why not take advantage of this newfound family environment? It would make a wonderful change in her life and form pleasant memories for the years to come.

"Say, I didn't think my getting a haircut would be cause for this much consideration." Matt's teasing drawl broke through her reverie.

A growing intensity of anxious voices filtered in from the hallway. Both Kit and Matt quickly responded to Teresa's flustered call. When they arrived in the large center foyer, they found the tiny housekeeper clutching a large stack of mail, surrounded by a collection of boxes. Five large cartons were from Cutter Bill's Western Wear and twelve pristine white boxes carried the embossed imprint of Elegant Rags, an exclusive designer shop in the Paseo del Rio.

"What is all this?" Matt inquired, relieving Teresa of the banded collection of mail and eyeing the deliveries.

"Everyone arrived at once." Teresa threw her hands in the air in unaccustomed agitation. "The delivery men, they said all these were for you, Kit," she explained, looking to the redhead for confirmation.

"Me?" Kit's smooth forehead creased in puzzlement. "I didn't order anything. I can't even afford to window-shop at these two stores."

Matt opened the largest box, whistled, and handed Kit a brown, snub-toed leather boot with an intricate ten-row stitch pattern. From a round hatbox he passed her a sleek black Spanish riding hat.

Kit's face hardened into granite, and a muscle moved ominously in her cheek. Slowly she opened the boxes, remembering Rafe's gibe of making this masquerade worth her while. She unwrapped dresses, blouses, skirts, and jeans, each bearing the unmistakable stamp of couturier excellence. As her fingers flipped open the smallest of the white boxes, she gave an audible gasp, slapped the lid closed, and tucked it under a protective arm.

Her lungs jerkily breathed in as she tried to control her anger. The absolute nerve of that man!

At the sound of the telephone, Kit's eyes narrowed into dangerously gleaming slits. "I'll get it," she announced, the menacing tone of her voice halting Teresa's automatic response. She scooped the bundle of mail from the hallway credenza and ran into the den, where she took in a deep controlling breath before her fingers curved in a stranglehold around the gold receiver.

"Well, this is a pleasant surprise." Rafe's voice was low and husky in her ear. "How's everything going?"

Kit looked up and found both Matt and Teresa framed in the doorway. Now that she had acquired an audience, she had no alternative but to play the loving fiancée. Using supreme self-control, she pasted a deceptively sweet smile on her face and slid her lithe form into the desk chair. "Everything is just wonderful," she cooed, honey dripping from her voice.

"Hmm. You sound remarkably like the kitten that ate a canary," he said in his lazy drawl. "What have you been up to this morning?"

Not quite as much as you, Kit thought slyly. "Actually," she purred, her eyes studying the intricate stucco swirls on the ceiling, "I've been working on the clinic project all morning. I'll have some letters for your approval when you get home."

"Say, you don't have to put in eight hours behind the desk," Rafe returned quickly. "Spend the afternoon in the pool or take another ride on Zodiac." He paused, his voice turning smooth as glass. "Of course, the sun might be too much for you without a hat."

Kit chuckled silently, her fingers drumming lightly on the desk top. "Don't worry about me," she answered blithely, "I'm just fine."

Rafe cleared his throat. "Anything interesting arrive today?" he asked casually.

"Oh, you mean the mail," she returned, being deliberately obtuse. Her fingers pushed aside the rubber band and her eyes sorted the contents. "You got six magazines, the telephone bill, and three envelopes marked 'occupant.' "

"Was that all?"

Kit smiled at the odd inflection in his voice. "Were you expecting anything else?" she asked innocently. She winked happily when she caught Matt's wide grin and smiled encouragingly at Teresa's confused expression.

"No." Rafe breathed a heavy sigh. "Kit, I'm afraid I won't be home for dinner. I've had a business meeting on my calendar for a month and there's no way I can break it."

"That's all right." The creative wheels in her brain began to whirl, and a slow smile lit her face. "What time do you think you'll be home?" she inquired pleasantly.

"It could be quite late. Will you wait up for me?" The husky timbre of his voice had a disturbing effect on Kit. She wiggled uncomfortably in the chair.

"I'm sure I'll be seeing you before the evening's over," she answered silkily before slipping the receiver back on its hook.

Kit pursed her lips, staring contemptuously at the silent instrument, the tempo of her still drumming fingers increasing in direct proportion to her burning animosity.

Matt sauntered over to the desk, attempted to peek into the small white gift box, and was rewarded with a sharp slap on the wrist. Kit raised a triumphant gaze and smiled, a smile that did not reach her silvery eyes. "Grab some of those boxes, Matthew," she ordered crisply. "Teresa, put lunch on hold."

"You want these all down at your cottage?" Matt inquired, following her into the foyer.

She shook her head. "No, the master bedroom," Kit announced bluntly. "According to the address labels, this nifty little wardrobe was designated for R. Morgan, and R. Morgan will find them hanging in his closet."

"But . . . but, Senorita Kit," Teresa stammered, twisting her hands nervously, "the delivery men, they said this was all for you."

"But I didn't order these things, Teresa." She sighed and gave the small woman an affectionate hug. "Don't worry. Rafe will have no doubts who arranged this."

Teresa shuffled back into the kitchen muttering what sounded to Kit like a Spanish prayer. She grinned at Matt and started piling boxes into his outstretched arms. Together they mounted the carved staircase, following the beige carpet to the master bedroom.

"Are you going to want any help?" Matt inquired, carefully lowering his parcels on the chocolate-brown spread that covered the king-size bed.

Kit shook her head. "Ignorance is bliss." She directed an accusing glance at him, reached out, and pulled a shaggy lock of sandy hair. "Weren't you going to get this cut?"

Matt laughed and headed for the door. "I've got an idea what you're up to and I'm sure we'll all hear Uncle Rafe's roar later tonight." He tossed her an admiring salute and went whistling down the stairs.

Kit stood in the center of the enormous bedroom suite admiring the handsome carved Mediterranean furnishings and the rich gold, toast, and cream decor that echoed the rest of the house. The room was large enough to include a twin cream satin love seat conversation area, a wall of bookcases, a writing desk, and a glass and chrome liquor cart. Behind the voluptuous wall of drapes were French doors that led to a screened sleeping porch.

Off to the right was one of the most elegant bathrooms she had ever seen outside of a decorating magazine. A crystal chandelier shimmered over a sunken tub, complete with Jacuzzi, that resembled a small swimming pool. There were a sauna and a separate shower. The room's fixtures were in gold, crystal, and Italian marble.

Kit's feet sank ankle-deep into the carpeting as she walked back across the bedroom and found what she was looking for: a wall of louvered doors that opened to reveal a massive closet. It had obviously been designed for two, and Rafe had most considerately left one half completely empty.

An hour later, her shoulders aching and her fingers marked for life from the weight of the metal hangers, Kit wondered if this was really worth the effort. She stretched, stepped back, and admired her handiwork. A frankly feminine array of clothing swung airily in what had previously been a very masculine wardrobe.

She walked back to the bed and opened the remaining small box. Of all the clothes, this proved to be the most baffling purchase. Pushing the tissue covering aside, Kit lifted out a teal-blue sleep teddy.

The ridiculously feminine piece of sheer lingerie had a lacy, plunging décolletage, a satin inset, and high French-cut legs.

Kit stared at the blatantly sensuous nightwear. She could understand his purchasing the riding gear; she could even tolerate the additional clothing. But not this. Her cold fingers crushed the warm silken material in a grip of steel. If this was Rafe Morgan's subtle message to inform her of other expected duties, then he had sorely miscalculated.

She might suffer from serious character faults, but her morals had not dissipated low enough to turn her into a prostitute like . . . She shook her head sharply and returned to the closet.

The riding boots stood in polished attention on the floor, the hat sat complacently on the top shelf, and she hung the suggestive teddy in the center of the other clothes. Kit slid the louvered doors shut and taped a carefully penned note on the varnished wood. She had no doubt that she, too, would hear an angry roar when Rafe Morgan returned home!

"Time may fly when you're having fun," Kit grumbled to Nosey, "but minutes go by like hours when you're waiting for the guillotine to fall!" The silvery schnauzer, exhausted from his attempts to wriggle free, finally ceased struggling and let Kit administer flea spray and a good brushing. Nosey then rolled back onto his feet, gave himself a complete head-to-tail shake, and sneezed. Kit laughed and patted the sofa cushion. The dog needed no second invitation to join her.

She had spent the rest of the afternoon typing the final version of the bid letters to six hospital supply companies and had helped Teresa plan the weekly menu. Matt had returned from town, not only with a new hairstyle but a few new clothes as well.

Kit had suffered his teasing through a delicious veal dinner and four games of Scrabble, all of which she had lost. Her mind was totally preoccupied with listening for the sound of Rafe's Porsche rather than with creating words from tile letters.

It was nearly eleven when Kit tossed Agatha Christie aside, not caring whether Miss Marple ever found out who dun it. Waiting had always been nerve-racking. It brought back memories of standing before numerous school principals to face up to assorted high crimes and misdemeanors.

Maybe a cup of tea would relax her. Kit pushed herself off the sofa, wiping clammy hands on the nubby material of her white terry jump suit. She filled a tiny Pyrex kettle with one cup of water and set it on the two-burner stove unit. Her eyes angrily ordered the water to boil.

Surely a business dinner wouldn't go on this long. Impatiently, she poured the lukewarm liquid into a mug. Of course, she thought ruefully, her fingers squeezing the dripping tea bag against the side of the china cup, Rafe could have met someone after dinner. Someone dainty and feminine; someone enticing and sensuous; someone who was the perfect model for that lacy teddy hanging in his closet. He might not come home tonight at all!

Kit dragged herself back to the sofa, curled her long legs under her, and sipped the warm beverage. The guest cottage was dark, save for the glow of the reading lamp. The decorative Casablanca-style ceiling fan hummed softly. She had disdained the use of air conditioning, throwing open all the windows and letting the fan provide a cooling breeze.

Finished with her tea, Kit rested her head against the plush sofa cushion, her fingers gently massaging Nosey's furry ears. The half-sleeping dog stretched all four legs and uttered a contented sigh. The warm drink, the gentle breeze, and the whirl of the fan blades hypnotically lulled Kit into a contented lethargy.

Both she and Nosey literally fell off the couch at the sound of Rafe's ominous bellow. Kit's hand leapt to her breast, trying to keep her madly pounding heart from jumping out of her chest. She swallowed the wildly beating pulse lodged in her throat.

Her name was roared again. She suddenly felt the need for action. Her long legs carried her out the back door into the pool area. She tucked herself behind one of the striped cabanas and cursed the nearly full gibbous moon for robbing her haven of shadows.

"Kit!" She peeked out from her shelter and saw Rafe framed in the open doorway. His shirt was completely unbuttoned and pulled free of his trousers. Nosey was playfully jumping at the loosely hanging material. The moonlight cast his rugged features in forbidding harsh angles. "Go on and find her, boy," he ordered the excitedly dancing schnauzer.

Kit groaned silently. She had forgotten about Nosey. Hearing his paws tap-dancing across the concrete, she looked around, spied a metal ashtray, and skittered it across the patio. Both dog and master turned in the opposite direction.

Quietly, she edged around the rear of the cabana, circling behind Rafe, who had stopped at the edge of the pool, muttering dire threats to her person. "Tut-tut! Such language!" she scolded, boldly making her presence known.

Rafe whirled, ready to bag his quarry, only to find himself held at bay with the long aluminum handle of the pool skimmer Kit had hastily confiscated.

He folded his long arms across his broad chest and took a deep breath. "What the hell is the matter with you?" His voice cracked through the silent night like a whip.

A pair of luminous blue eyes blinked wide and innocent. "Not a blessed thing."

"Then will you kindly tell me why you rearranged my closet?"

"To make room for your new wardrobe," she returned with cheerful impudence.

"You know damn well those clothes were for you," Rafe exploded, his nostrils flaring angrily.

"Oh, no. There was one thing I did manage to learn. A gift accepted is a gift beholden." Her voice was firm and clear. "When I leave here, Rafe Morgan, I'm going to make damn sure I don't owe you a thing!"

His eyes narrowed dangerously, his mouth grim. Rafe dropped his arms and took a step forward, only to be effectively halted by a sharp jab from the pole she was wielding. "And who taught you how to write such nasty, sarcastic notes?" he demanded contemptuously.

"Don't you dare accuse me of being insulting!" she charged, her eyes flashing spiritedly, every muscle in her body tensed rebelliously. "You've got some nerve! I'm the one who's been insulted, especially by that ridiculous piece of lingerie," she retorted defensively.

Rafe's hand came up, rubbing his face reflectively. "Actually, it reminded me of you." He grinned unrepentantly, his teeth flashing with undisguised amusement.

"Me?" Kit snorted her disgust. "That tiny, fragile, lacy thing?" Her brow arched cynically, knowing she did not at all fit that description.

Rafe laughed. "Well, they say brevity is the soul of wit, and you are the wittiest thing I have ever come across." He gave her his most charming smile, his voice low and cajoling. "Come on, Kit, take the clothes. You can use them. You need the riding gear."

"I need nothing from you," she returned coldly. "I've survived very well without help from anyone."

"That's just the point, dammit. You're not supposed to be surviving, you're supposed to be living and enjoying life."

"If you think it takes beautiful, expensive clothes to do that, Rafe Morgan, then . . . then . . ."—her eyes glittered wickedly and a smile played on her lips—"then you're all wet!" Kit put all of her considerable strength against the aluminum pole, easily toppling a startled Rafe Morgan into the pool with a resounding splash.

She dropped the pole and started to laugh, pushing a barking, jumping Nosey off her leg. Abruptly, her laughter died when Rafe failed to surface.

Kit swallowed hard and dropped to her knees, peering into the dark water of the huge pool. "Rafe? Rafe!" Her voice was urgent as she tried to calculate how long he had been under the water. If he was teasing, she'd kill him. But what if he wasn't? What if he had hit his head? What if he couldn't swim? A chaotic jumble of thoughts whirled through her mind.

Kit wiped her lips nervously, looking up at the sky, willing the cloud that had blocked out most of the moon to move. In her panic, she forgot about the switch for the pool lights. "Rafe!" she yelled, leaning far out over the water.

A pair of wet hands snaked up and gripped her wrists, yanking her off balance and tumbling her into the warm water. Those same strong hands returned her to the surface seconds later. Spluttering and gasping for air, Kit leaned against Rafe's broad chest, blinking water from her eyes.

A furiously barking Nosey, thinking they were playing some kind of new game, leapt into the air, landing with a resounding shower of water at their side. Kit brushed sodden strands of hair off her face with a dripping hand. Her gaze swung from the madly paddling dog to her grinning companion. She couldn't contain the growing bubble of laughter that rose in her throat. The tension had been broken, leaving Kit alive, warm, and energized.

"You scared me," she charged. "I thought you had drowned." She playfully directed a spray of water at him.

"It serves you right," Rafe returned easily, his arms wrapped around her waist, pulling her body against his in the shoulder-high water. "You are the most stubborn, obstinate, willful, headstrong—"

"But witty," she teasingly interrupted, her hands splayed across his chest, her fingers tangling in an enticing mat of wet, dark hair.

"Very witty," he murmured huskily, the grooves deepening in his cheeks, his dark gaze searching her upturned face.

Kit had meant to slip out of his grasp and swim away, but the intoxicating feel of his hard body so closely entwined with her own sapped her resistance. Unconsciously, she leaned forward, resting against him, her full breasts soft against his hard chest. Her blue eyes were held captive by his magnetic brown ones. Rafe's mouth lowered over hers, hungrily parting her lips, tasting, exploring, and devouring her with savage abandon.

Kit's water-soaked jump suit relinquished its protective duties under his passionate caresses. Her skin felt naked to his exploring hands. She moaned against his lips, feeling her breasts and nipples harden under the gentle teasing of his skilled fingers. His leg slid intimately between her thighs, making her all too aware of a growing ache inside her and of a shared physical need.

It was a dangerous physical delight. The provocative mastery of his touch spread molten fire through her veins. For the first time in her life, she felt feminine and desirable. Her body instinctively responded to him.

"You're purring like a kitten," he murmured against her throat, the hairs of his mustache tickling her ear.

The sound of his voice dissolved the magic. Kit's muscles tensed. The critical voice in her mind rang out loud and clear. Rafe was using her, experimenting with her emotions. A sexual exchange for recreational purposes. After all, she was simply a substitute, a standby for the real love of his life.

Confused and bitter, she slipped out of his arms. In three easy strokes she reached the pool ladder and climbed out. Rafe turned slowly, shaking his head in surprise. He guided the still-swimming dog to the ladder. After lifting Nosey safely onto the patio, he levered his powerful body next to hers. "Kit?" Rafe inquired softly. His long fingers captured her chin and turned her averted face toward him.

"I'll only go so far in my act as your *loving* fiancée," she told him coldly.

He raised a dark brow, studying her impassive features in the moonlight. "That's just fine," Rafe said slowly. "You know that old saying: The night has a thousand eyes?" Kit nodded, her smooth forehead puckering in confusion. "I just wanted to make sure anyone watching would realize we had stopped fighting." He favored her with another one of his wide, dimpled grins.

Her lips twisted in a wry, disbelieving smile. She ran her hands over her head, squeezing the water from her saturated hair.

"What do you want me to do with the new clothes?" Rafe asked, his eyes leisurely enjoying the unhampered view of her body the nearly transparent jump suit afforded.

"Do you really want me to tell you?" she parried facetiously. When she caught the direction of his gaze, she sighed exasperatedly and rearranged her position.

Rafe grinned, enjoying her discomfort. "You will take the riding gear."

She shook her head.

"Damn it, Kit, you need the boots and the hat,"

he exploded, unable to keep his temper in check. Rafe exhaled forcefully. Pulling off his own water-logged boots, he laid them on the tile rim of the pool. "I could put a halt to your riding," he warned dangerously. Stripping off his sodden shirt, he turned and tossed it toward a deck chair.

Kit choked on her flip reply, her eyes riveted to the thick network of raised keloid scars gleaming against his otherwise smooth torso. "Rafe?" The word came out a whispered question. Unconsciously she reached out, her fingers gently touching the vicious burn residue.

"A little bon voyage present from the Vietcong," he said calmly, extremely conscious of her stricken face. "Does it bother you?"

Kit swallowed and shook her head. "The pain must have nearly killed you," she breathed, her eyes blinking rapidly against a burning sensation.

"They told me I screamed like hell before I passed out," he reported rather cheerfully.

She closed her eyes and shuddered. "I'm sorry." It seemed the only appropriate thing to say, but somehow sounded shallow and silly. How could anyone apologize for a war?

Kit's eyes fluttered open when she felt his hands on her face. "Sometimes the scars that don't show are the ones that hurt the worst."

Rafe's statement surprised her. He seemed to be reaching out to her. His expression was serious, but his eyes were warm and inviting. Kit felt herself

101

shrinking away. Risking any type of intimacy, verbal or physical, was as frightening as facing your own personal conflicts. She pulled herself out of his grasp and jumped to her feet. "I'll buy the riding hat. Leave the bill on the desk."

She refused to acknowledge his call. Instead, she turned and hurried into the safety of the cottage and locked the door.

CHAPTER FIVE

Kit swallowed the sour taste forming in her mouth and sullenly eyed the pastel pink envelope that had arrived with the morning mail. The letter bore a New York postmark; the writing was in a lacy feminine script; and the scent of one-hundred-dollar-an-ounce Joy that permeated the stationery made it all too clear who the sender was. It had taken Tracy Shippley less than a week to take up the gauntlet for reclaiming Rafe Morgan.

During that week, Kit had been able to relax despite finding herself more deeply entrenched in a family situation. Rafe had been called away to the oil fields near Del Rio, which accounted for her lessening tensions. He had, however, left her and Matt in charge of the ranch and given her full authority over the clinic project. Rafe had cleverly maneuvered her into handling all his personal bills and doing the ranch's paperwork by saying how much he hated accounting and how fortunate he had been to acquire a fiancée who excelled in bookkeeping.

Kit had pointedly ignored his provoking comments but she had agreed to handle the bookwork. Any further efforts on the clinic project were stalled until the finalization of the land acquisition, and she eagerly welcomed the extra tasks to keep her busy.

Teresa had been teaching her a variety of new recipes and cooking techniques. During the evenings she and Matt enjoyed playing cards or Scrabble and talking. She had noticed subtle changes in Matt. Gone was the surly, unkempt teen-age rebel. In his place was a responsible, level-headed adult, who was already studying for his college boards.

The ringing of the telephone brought Kit back to her immediate duties. She was surprised to hear Rafe on the line. "How's everything at the rigs?" she inquired pleasantly, her tone betraying none of the emotions that flooded her body just from hearing his deep voice.

"I finished up early this morning. I'm back here at the office," he told her pleasantly. "How's everything with you?"

"Just fine. Matt is checking the tack order that just arrived. Yesterday he moved a small herd of Brangus to the high pasture, and we got one tenth of an inch of rain last night, which lowered the temperature to a mere ninety-eight." Kit broke into a wide grin. "You also got a feed bill that rivals the national debt."

Rafe laughed, a low husky sound that made her wriggle uncomfortably. "Anything else?" At a prolonged silence, she heard, "Kit!" It was an order.

She cleared her throat and squared her shoulders. After all, wasn't this what she was here for? "Your fish snapped the bait."

"I beg your pardon?"

"A letter arrived today from New York bearing the unmistakable stench—I mean scent—of Tracy Shippley," she reported sweetly.

"I see." Rafe paused. "Well, open it and let's see what she wants," he directed curtly.

"She wants *you*," Kit returned dryly. "And since it's likely to be highly personal, I think—"

"Since when do *I* have any secrets from you?" he interrupted smoothly. "Open it, Kit."

Grumbling her reluctance, she slit open the envelope and extracted two sheets of paper. Hesitantly, she began reading the flowing script. " 'My dearest darling.' " Kit wrinkled her nose. "Rafe," she moaned, "I really think you should—"

"Quit stalling, Kit," he ordered sharply. "Read the damn letter. I don't blush easily."

"Fine, fine," she snapped belligerently, her chin jutting out defensively at the words on the pastel stationery. "I think I'll read it in a rolling Southern drawl, just so you'll get the proper effect." She ignored his throaty chuckle, composed her features, and started reading in a voice dripping with a honeyed lilt. " 'My dearest darlin': I never realized just how much our quarrel had affected you until I heard about your sudden engagement. You must have been terribly wounded to seek such quick comfort.

" 'I was shocked to discover she is one of our employees and Marybeth tells me that she is totally opposite of what anyone would expect from you. This leads me to believe that this engagement is a mere temporary transgression on your part and will be terminated once you know how unsuitable Miss Forrester is.' " Kit's spine stiffened; her body went cold. Nervously she moistened her dry lips. Her voice lost its tart inflection, turning detached and flat.

" 'We felt it was our duty to acquaint you with all the facts. Even Daddy was quite surprised and we know just what a shock this would be to your mama. The entire family is trash.' " Kit stopped speaking and closed her eyes. She didn't have to read the facts; she had lived them. Tracy Shippley's venom-dipped pen could add no new poisons to a life best forgotten.

Her eyes once again focused on the letter. *Trash.* She had thought the very word herself, but somehow when it came from someone else it splintered against her throat like a bone, sharp and indigestible.

The growing urgency of Rafe's voice yelling in her ear went unheeded. She simply disconnected him.

Kit stared at the letter with contempt for the woman who wrote it. A chaotic jumble of emotions gripped her. She grew angry and resentful. The past was like flypaper; it never left you. It was forever tangling itself with the present and bent on disrupting the future. The cruel reality of her life would always be within her. Over the years she had made up little stories—lies—about her parents and her childhood and had begun to believe them. There was no way of escaping the truth. It turned up like the proverbial bad penny. Her trembling hands raked through her fall of copper hair.

Tracy Shippley had written the truth. She must love Rafe very much. When you love someone, you want only the best for them. The normally spacious confines of the den grew suffocatingly close, stealing Kit's very breath.

Her body was screaming for action, for some way to rid itself of the growing turbulence and intense anxiety that erupted from every pore. Kit sprang from the chair, startling a sleeping Nosey, and lunged for the door. She slammed into Matt, recklessly pushing him aside in her haste to escape. Her hands covered her ears, shutting out the persistently ringing telephone, the dog's flustered barking, and Matt's plaintive calls.

Fifteen minutes later, both she and Zodiac were lathered by their vigorous ride and the heat of the blazing sun. She reined the snorting stallion into a more controlled gait, letting the horse pick his way through the rocky terrain of a dry creek bed as she guided him toward a tree-sheltered oasis a few yards farther on.

Kit sat on a large boulder, her copper head cradled in her folded arms. Her cold blue eyes watched the unceasing energies of a swarm of ants building their trampled home. The ants, she sensed dully, seemed infinitely more adept at reconstruction than humans. Each ant silently carried out its assigned task with the strength of Atlas. They lived and worked with each other in a colony. Hunting, feeding, guarding, and caring for the young. Here were insects, the lowest form of crawling life, enjoying the one thing she had never had—a home.

In a blind rage, Kit lifted her sandaled foot and crushed what was left of the anthill. She kicked out at the dry scrub grass and the rock-strewn earth, trying to purge herself of years of repressed hostility that boiled through her veins.

A most puzzled "What on earth are you doing?" made her whirl around in surprise. It was Matt, astride his wide-backed Appaloosa, a whimpering Nosey draped over his saddle.

"Haven't you ever seen a person throw a temper tantrum before?" Kit replied coldly. She shook her head. Her strength suddenly seemed to desert her. She reached up and took possession of the panting dog, watching Matt tether Thor to the same tree as Zodiac. "What are you doing here?" she asked, her tired body collapsing on a flat boulder.

"You're throwing a fit; Rafe's throwing a fit; even the damn dog was throwing a fit," Matt raged defensively in a minifit of his own. He stopped yelling and stared at her slumped figure with compassionate brown eyes. "I read that bitch's letter. I don't know why you're so upset over a pack of lies. She's just jealous. Rafe is—"

"They are not a pack of lies." Kit enunciated each word slowly and distinctly. She set a calmer Nosey on the ground and turned toward Matt, her blue eyes level and direct. "Every word in the letter Tracy wrote is the truth."

"Wait a minute. You can't . . . I mean . . . I don't . . . " he stammered incredulously, his brown gaze hazy in confusion.

Kit's fingers gently massaged the tension from her forehead. She looked at his concerned face, exhaled a long breath, and patted the stone seat beside her. "There is no greater fallacy than saying youth is your happiest time of life. Mine was hell. You've spent hours complaining to me about how your family is always on your back, never giving you any space. Your parents want to know what you're doing and whom you're doing it with. They demand that you finish high school and go to college. They're always after you, you told me; they never leave you alone.

"That, Matt Bishop, is love. Your parents love and care about you. They brought you into this world and are trying to make sure you're well equipped to handle whatever life deals you." Kit patted his arm and stood up. She stared out at the grassy, rough terrain, searching for something: the strength to tell the truth.

"My parents were alcoholics. They lived in a fun-filled, blurred existence until I was born. A baby meant responsibility, and neither of them wanted that. They shoved me on my grandmother, who didn't relish having a baby either. She never liked my father and she transferred that dislike to me.

"Kids are not stupid, Matt, and unfortunately I was bright . . . bright enough to recognize her feelings. Since I was being treated like trash, I started acting the part. I was a hellion, and as soon as she could, my grandmother dumped me into one strict parochial school after another, hoping the fear of God would straighten me out. It didn't. I had more rulers broken across my backside and saw the inside of more closets—" She shook her head, her eyes focusing on the smooth collection of stones that peppered the ground.

"After my grandmother died, I went home. Home?" The word was strangled in her throat. "A home is full of love and warmth. I went to a house, shingles and clapboard hammered together with hate." She took a deep breath. "My parents were always fighting, and having me around only made things worse. Soon the neighbors were calling the police, one or both were arrested, and I would temporarily be sent to one of those juvenile holding tanks. Which was exactly where I belonged."

110

Kit's face twisted in mocking self-derision. "I was a mess. Physically, mentally, emotionally. So full of anger and hate. I could have easily succumbed to drugs or turned into a teen-age runaway and ended up a hooker, but I didn't. I was strong and tough and flexible. Like a fighter, I rolled with the punches, building a steel coat of armor around my emotions. I made up little stories and convinced myself that, like Cinderella, some nice fairy godmother would come and take me away. I'm still waiting for her to show up."

Kit bent over, her long fingers curling around a small rock. Its surface was smooth from countless years of exposure to the elements. How wonderful if time could smooth away memories the way Nature had worn away the stone. "I was your age when my father left. Later we were notified that he had been killed in a car accident—drunken driving. I continued living with my mother. I had the Fifth Commandment drilled into me for so long that I really believed things might get better between us, that she might start liking her daughter. But she didn't. She was getting older and more depressed. She started taking in men." Kit cleared her throat. "I guess she thought it would boost her morale. She was arrested for prostitution." She licked her dry lips, forcing herself to continue.

"I tried to stay out of the house, out of her way. But sometimes, well . . . you hear things, they stay with you, and emotionally I was retarded and crippled. Anyway, she got a little careless and mixed pills with gin for breakfast and . . ." Her voice trailed off. "It took me years to pull myself together, to even get to a stage where I like myself, just a little. I was so excited about moving to Texas, coming west, starting a new life, meeting new people, being judged for myself."

Her eyes slid to the rock still gripped in her hand. She threw it and watched it disappear in the distance. How easy that was. How much more difficult it was to fling away the past. Kit shivered under the cold hand of Fate. She had no right associating with these people, living in their world of luxury, enjoying the fruits born from yet another one of her lies. This would end the masquerade. Rafe would be pleased at the ease with which the web had been untangled. Tracy Shippley would return and assume her rightful role.

Kit hazarded a glance at Matt. He was just sitting, staring at his clenched hands. He had been quiet for so long, she was positive she had lost his regard, too. She walked over and stood in front of him. "Matt, let's go back to the ranch. I want to pack and leave. I—"

"You know"—his head snapped up and he looked at her with suspiciously moist dark eyes—"for someone I thought was smart and together, you can be remarkably stupid at times." He stood up, his hands settling heavily on her shoulders, giving them a comforting squeeze. "You have nothing to be ashamed of. You were a victim. Tracy Shippley is about as pleasant as a tablespoon of castor oil. Her whole life revolves around the size of a bank balance, ancestral lineage, and the designer label on the seat of her jeans."

She smiled at him, her hand gently brushing back a fallen lock of sandy hair. "I'm going to miss you."

"Miss me?" he echoed. "You're not going anyplace, and I'm here for another month. Listen, you didn't hear Uncle Rafe on the phone. He was mad all right, but not at you."

Kit turned away. What could she tell him? Her position as Rafe's fiancée was solely a ploy to make Tracy jealous. "I know all about Rafe and Tracy," she said slowly, her gaze focusing on Nosey's zealous digging into a prairie dog's hole. "She loves him and only wants the best for him. I'm not it."

Matt looked uncomfortable. "I'm not sure what Tracy wants, but I can't believe you're not going to fight."

"Fight?" She looked at him and laughed. "Shall I start another Trojan War? In this case, everything is left to Rafe."

He grinned ruefully. "Well, then let him decide." Matt slung an arm around her shoulders. "Come on, it's hotter than hell out here, and your face is beginning to compete with your hair."

Together they walked to their horses. Kit mounted Zodiac and found Nosey barking anxiously up at

113

her. "Give him to me, Matt," she directed, steadying the pawing stallion with a calm hand.

"I don't know, Kit." Matt eyed the nervous horse dubiously. "Zodiac is more spirited and sensitive than Thor. He's not used to dogs."

"We'll be fine," she assured him, and sliding back against the cantle, she settled the dog's quivering body over the saddle fork. One hand held the reins, the other balanced the silver schnauzer. Kit let her legs and feet guide Zodiac back across the rugged terrain.

Nosey looked with interest at the moving ground below. When his alert brown eyes spotted the speedy movements of a speckled collared lizard, he gave a high-pitched bark, his back legs scrambling against the leather stirrup fender. Zodiac reared back, pawing the air in alarm. Kit vainly struggled to control both the horse and the dog.

The massive stallion wheeled sideways as Nosey lunged from under Kit's arm and leapt for his quarry. Her sandals slipped off the flat metal stirrups, letting them thump against the horse's ribs. Zodiac broke into a frightened gallop. Kit, the reins tangled around her wrist, lost her seat and found herself pulled through the sharp underbrush and over the jagged landscape. Precious seconds went by before she freed herself and hit the ground with the full impact of her weight.

She lay still for a moment, staring into the blurred,

114

fiery sun. Her heart was pounding against her ribs; her breath was coming in painful, jerky gulps.

Matt's horrified face loomed into focus. "Kit! My God, you could have been killed." He was alternately swearing and praying as he helped her sit up, his shaky fingers gently brushing the dirt from her grazed cheek.

"I'm still in one piece." She coughed, trying to ignore the deafening roar in her ears. Experimentally, she slowly began to move various parts of her bruised body. Her feet and legs responded normally; the pain in her chest was rapidly dissipating, and her head was beginning to clear. She flexed her arms, letting out a sharp yelp when a million needles stabbed at her back and shoulders.

Matt moved and winced. "It's your back. Your blouse is torn to shreds."

"Never mind the blouse," Kit ordered, keeping her torso completely rigid. "What does my body look like?"

Gingerly, he finished ripping the thin material of her madras shirt. His teeth gnawed his lower lip as he carefully brushed away the dirt, gravel, and dust to expose the raw bleeding skin. "I think it looks worse than it really is. There are a few deep gouges, but it's mostly surface scratches. It's going to hurt like hell, and you'll need a tetanus shot."

She exhaled thankfully. "Don't worry about the tetanus shot. I had one a few months ago when a skateboarder collided with my bike." She crawled to her feet, leaning heavily on Matt's arm. "Let's get back to the ranch. I think a two-hour soak in a tub and plenty of antiseptic and I'll be good as new."

She declined Matt's offer of his shirt, letting him tie the two ripped halves of her blouse together. Slowly and stiffly she approached Zodiac, ruefully eyeing the saddle, which loomed abnormally high off the ground. "It looks like the Himalayas." She grinned, gratefully accepting help to mount.

Nosey whimpered and crawled on his belly. "We should let him walk back." Matt eyed the dog with disgust. Then he scooped him up and settled him over Thor's saddle.

The trip back to the ranch was an exercise in endurance for Kit. Every muscle and joint in her body was screaming in pain. She was stiff and sore, her back felt sticky with blood and drenched with perspiration, and the relentlessly beating sun was hammering her uncovered head into a throbbing mass.

She literally fell into Matt's arms when she dismounted. "I'm taking a bottle of aspirin and a gallon of cold water and going to quietly drown in the bathtub." She groaned, letting him assist her into the guest cottage.

"Are you sure you don't want me to call the doctor?" Matt persisted, anxiously eyeing her sunburned raw back.

"No. Once all this dirt and blood soaks off and I put some antiseptic on, I'll be fine." Kit gave him a wobbly smile before dragging herself into the lavender bathroom.

She dumped half a box of mineral crystals she found in the cupboard into the deep, old-fashioned tub and filled it with the hottest water she could tolerate. It was a painful task to strip off the remnants of her blouse, and she literally bit her lip in agony when she reached back to unhook her bra.

Stepping out of her filthy jeans, Kit viewed her naked body in the full-length wall mirror. Green and purple bruises were beginning to form on her legs and buttocks. From her shoulder blades to her waist was a disgusting area of dirt, blood, and loose skin.

She switched on the whirlpool attachment and eased her body into the chin-high swirling water. Giving a long sigh of relief, she closed her eyes and let the machine whip the water into a frothy mass of soothing comfort that was already salving her aching body.

CHAPTER SIX

The unmistakable, authoritative sound of boots on tile caused Kit's eyelids to open in alarm. She found herself staring up into Rafe Morgan's grim face. Instinctively, her body shrank lower into the vibrating, sudsy water.

"What do you want?" she asked irritably, eyeing his tall, commanding figure, clad in jeans and a denim workshirt, which towered over her.

"I came to assess the damages."

"They're practically healed."

"This is Texas, not Lourdes," Rafe countered dryly, sinking to his haunches, his brown gaze leveled straight into her blue eyes. "Sit up and let me see your back."

"I can tend to it myself," she insisted stubbornly,

pressing her spine into the enamel of the tub. "It's not that bad."

"That's not what Matt told me," he stated forcefully, one dark brow arched sardonically. "Drop the modest maiden act. You've got nothing I haven't seen before."

"Complimentary to the end, aren't you?" Kit said, smirking nastily. "I don't need or want your help." Each word was clear and hard, as was the stony gaze she leveled at his face.

Rafe smiled and slowly rolled up the sleeves of his blue workshirt. "It's going to be a pleasure coming in after you, honey."

"I wouldn't want you and your gold watch to drown," she warned sharply, sliding her body against the far side of the old-fashioned claw-footed tub.

"We're both waterproof to two hundred feet."

"Rafe!" Kit yelped in panic at the touch of his powerful, dry fingers curving around her wet, soapy shoulders. She hastily planted a dripping hand flat against his chest in a tentative effort to hold him at bay. "If you would allow me a few minutes of privacy, I will be glad to dry off so you can play doctor," she told him in a calm tone.

He looked into her impassive features for a long moment, stood up, and walked to the door. "I'll be charitable and give you five minutes."

The prolonged soak in the whirlpool had had a therapeutic effect on both her body and her morale.

The cuts on her back were warm and moist, and she had little difficulty in moving her arms and shoulders. Kit wrapped an amethyst towel skirt-fashion around her slender waist, fastening the ends securely with a large safety pin. She tucked another towel under her arms; it left her back bare but covered her breasts. She was in no mood for another lecture on modesty but neither could she deny the fact that having Rafe Morgan in such close proximity caused considerable turbulence to her usually stable emotions.

True to his word, without even the preamble of knocking, Rafe pushed open the door, a first-aid kit tucked under his arm. Her blue eyes collided with his set features and wavered nervously. "It's really not that bad," she assured him, sitting down on the edge of the padded orchid vanity seat.

A muscle moved ominously in his cheek; his eyes glittered angrily while they surveyed her back. "Stop trying to pretend it doesn't hurt," he grated sharply. His fingers gently removed thin sheets of loose skin curling around the abrasions on an otherwise satiny back. Not a muscle moved or a nerve shuddered, as Rafe studied the dispassionate face reflected in the mirror. "This tells me a lot," he sighed heavily.

Kit swallowed at the slight sting of the antiseptic he was applying to her skin. "Why did you come home?" she asked hesitantly, her fingers idly tracing the swirl pattern on the towel.

"I was worried that you might do something rash and try to leave."

"Grand auto theft was not among my crimes," she returned acidly. She was silent for a moment, her teeth gnawing at the tender skin on the inside of her lower lip. "Did you . . . did you read the rest of Tracy's letter?"

"I didn't have to read it. I already knew about it," he said calmly, tipping more hydrogen peroxide onto his gauze pad.

"You . . . you knew?" she spluttered, her wide-eyed gaze snagging his in the mirror.

Rafe's voice was savage but the hands on her flesh were gentle. "That's right. I knew everything. What did you expect?" he asked brusquely. "I get a call congratulating me on acquiring a fiancée. Some person I've never even heard of. My first instinct was to see what kind of badger game I was being set up for, and believe me, your record didn't look good." He capped the antiseptic and surveyed his handiwork. "When I met you at Shippley's that night and found you were more surprised by me than I was with you, I was sure you weren't involved in any kind of blackmail scheme."

He folded his arms across his broad chest and leaned back against the vanity. "I've given you several opportunities to talk to me and tell me the truth. But no. I get bits and pieces. I get half-truths and lacy little lies. I have to hear the real story from Matt. You talk to him, but you keep shutting me out.

121

You keep everything to yourself, locked away, pretending you don't feel pain or pleasure." Rafe heard her sharp intake of breath and grinned. "Go ahead, tell me what you're thinking. Say it. You're just ready to erupt."

"What I'm thinking," Kit ground out sharply, "you can read off a bathroom wall, Rafe Morgan."

"Thatta girl, right back to normal," he laughed, patting her shoulder. "After you take a little nap, you'll be your usual bewitching self and the perfect hostess for our dinner guests tonight."

"Hostess! Dinner guests!" Kit yelled furiously. In one fluid angry movement she was off the stool, glaring at his amused, indolent expression. "You're crazy. I'm getting out of this looney tune today," she told him, her chin jutting out challengingly.

"The hell you are."

"The hell I'm not," she retorted spiritedly, her fingers stabbing sharply against his broad chest. She was completely oblivious to the fact that her towel had slipped, leaving her naked to the waist. "This works out perfectly for both of us. Tracy is ready to crawl back into your arms. I can leave and get on with my life. This whole damn charade comes to a quick, clean end."

Rafe's eyes narrowed into glowing agate slits. His hands closed over the soft skin of her upper arms, hauling her tightly against him. "I told you before, I call the shots. Tonight you are going to be the

122

loving, attentive fiancée everyone is waiting to meet. I am not ashamed of you."

Kit blinked and stared up at him in total confusion. He smiled, his hands sliding up to capture her face, pulling her trembling lips closer to his.

The potent touch of his mouth sent a channel of quicksilver sparking through her body. She leaned against him, enjoying the feel of his solid frame pressed against her soft contours. His lips moved to kiss her eyelids, her straight nose, her stubborn chin, traveling down the pulsating cord of her slender throat to her Adam's apple.

Her mind whirled amid a tumble of unspoken desires. With a soft sigh, she leaned her head back, the shimmering copper hair spilling like silk over his arm. Her fingers caressed the rough stubble of his unshaven cheek.

Kit stared into his half-hooded eyes bewilderedly. It would be so easy to let him absorb her. They were obviously sexually attracted to each other. She was losing her perspective. He didn't love her. She didn't love him. Playtime was getting mixed up with the real world.

Rafe surveyed her steadily, feeling the growing tension invade her previously pliant body. His fingers moved down her throat to lightly caress the sensitive tips of her breasts. He smiled lazily. "With that hair and body, you would have made a perfect model for Gauguin."

Gauguin, the painter of naked savages. Kit's color

rose uncontrollably. She pulled out of his embrace and quickly snatched up her fallen towel. "What time shall I be ready to great *our* guests?" she asked coldly, her features devoid of emotion.

"I'll walk down and get you at seven," Rafe announced. His face broke into a wide-dimpled grin, but she turned her back on him angrily, releasing a long-held breath only after she heard the door close.

Kit eyed herself critically in the mirror. Skillfully applied makeup had hidden the bruise on her cheek, another whirlpool bath had temporarily alleviated the stiffness in her sore muscles, and her dress for the evening seemed the perfect choice for mixing hostess and camouflage duties.

She had bought the deep aqua Spanish-style dress in the gift shop aboard the *Conquistador.* Its off-the-shoulder ruffled neckline, tiered skirt, and embroidered hemline added a dash of glamour, while the cool gauze material allowed air to circulate and dry the abrasions on her back. She regally acknowledged the compliment Rafe voiced but declined his offer of some special salve for her wounds.

"How many dinner guests are coming?" Kit queried while they walked across the rear patio to the main house.

"Three couples," Rafe replied, draping his arm lightly around her bare shoulders. "You've met two of them." At her puzzled expression, he grinned and answered her silent question. "Ted Vail, my attorney on the clinic project, is coming with his fiancée, Ginny Price. Jim Stanford and his wife, Gretchen—he's Stanford Development. And then Dr. John Demarest and his wife, Joan. John's one of the physicians on your consulting list for the hospital supply bids."

"The Shippleys aren't coming?" she asked hesitantly, waiting for him to open the back door.

His long fingers cupped her chin, snagging her anxious blue gaze with his own comforting brown eyes. "No. These are friends. Shippley is a business associate."

Kit was afforded no time to voice a reply as Matt and Teresa surrounded her with an onslaught of solicitous attention and concern. She went suddenly shy and awkward under the wake of such a display of genuine affection, feeling a sense of relief when the doorbell chimed.

All afternoon she had carefully prepared herself to face Rafe's dinner guests. She had schooled herself to expect an evening of sly, meaningful smiles and speculative stares. Instead, Kit abandoned her defensive attitude when she was once again the recipient of warmth and hospitality, which reminded her of the fact that the Indian word for friend was *Texas*.

Ted Vail had the keen eyes of an attorney set in a ruddy complexion. He was short and stocky but agile, both verbally and physically. His fiancée was an art teacher in the local elementary school. Ginny was petite with large brown eyes and elfin-cut black hair.

The Demarests were in their mid-forties. John was slim and angular, with gray hair and twinkling brown eyes. His wife, Joan, was a slender blond mother of three athletic boys.

Of all the couples, Kit found herself immediately drawn to the Stanfords. Gretchen not only matched her own Amazon proportions but possessed a self-assured wit that rivaled her own. Jim was a huge, amiable bear of a man whose resounding laughter echoed through the house.

Relaxing over cocktails and Teresa's delicious canapés, their conversation focused on the impending construction of the burn treatment clinic. Over a dinner of thick slabs of prime Texas beef with all the trimmings, a lively discussion of current events started and continued for the rest of the evening.

Kit had been worried about being ranked, rated, judged, and graded, but the only strain came from her aching body. Stiff, sore muscles painfully made their presence known. The skin on her back had dried and now cracked under even the slightest movement, causing her acute discomfort by the end of an otherwise pleasant evening.

Bidding their guests good night, Kit found herself scooped up in Jim Stanford's massive arms and given a bear hug of congratulations. Her eyes crossed as the tender flesh on her back split into a million screaming shreds.

When he finally released her, Kit literally crumpled into Rafe's waiting arms. "I'm going to faint," she announced, feeling a peculiar weakness invade her knees.

"No, you're not," he returned, easily taking her weight against his strong supportive body. They stood framed under the courtyard lights, watching the cars drive away. "Now, will you let me put on that salve?" Rafe asked gently, his fingers easing the strained lines of her face.

"I'd really rather die quietly in some dark corner," Kit sighed limply. She was too exhausted to extricate herself from the comfort and warmth of his arms. Mutely she let him guide her through the house, balking when they reached the staircase landing. She listlessly eyed the polished, curved banister and the fourteen carpeted steps. "I don't suppose your miracle cure could walk down here by itself?" she asked wearily, stifling a prodigious yawn with a limp hand.

An arm slid around her waist as another lifted her high against a muscular chest. She turned her startled gaze to meet Rafe's teasing brown eyes. "That's a good way to get a hernia," she cautioned dryly, automatically sliding her arms around his neck.

"I'll let you be the first to autograph my truss," he promised with a wide grin, effortlessly mounting the stairs.

"What is this mystery potion of yours anyway?" Kit asked with curiosity after being deposited on the edge of his wide bed.

"Actually, we made it up for the horses. It does wonders on pulled ligaments and cuts," he teased before disappearing into the bathroom. When he returned, he was carrying two jars, one filled with a clear liquid, the other with a thick yellow cream. "If you need any help getting out of that charming creation, just say the word," Rafe threatened lazily.

"I know, I know," Kit muttered, her fingers unbuttoning the blouson top of her dress. "When you've seen two, you've seen them all." The gauze material had glued itself to her uncovered lesions. Rafe immediately came to her rescue, deftly separating cloth from skin.

"You've really had quite a day, haven't you, sweetheart?" he said not unkindly, gently pushing her face down on the satiny brown spread. "Just relax, Dr. Morgan will fix you right up."

Kit burrowed her cheek into the softness of his bed pillows, inhaling the clinging masculine scent of Rafe's body. "What's that?" she asked, shivering against a cool trickle of liquid that dribbled onto her shoulders.

"That's the liniment," he said softly, his hands beginning to knead and massage her stiff, knotted muscles. "I couldn't help but notice you seemed to have an enjoyable evening."

"Hmm," Kit murmured, her lashes fluttering heavily onto her cheeks. "Your friends are nice."

"They're your friends too."

She barely heard him. The cool liniment was spreading a warm, relaxing glow across her flesh. Rafe's voice was growing fainter and more distant by the minute. Her mind and body dissolved into the soft comfort of the mattress.

Something warm and furry nuzzled her ear. "Nosey," Kit grumbled sleepily, "get off the bed."

"I didn't realize my shaving lotion smelled so animalistic."

The sound of a very amused, very familiar masculine voice brought immediate alertness to her sleep-dulled brain. Her pulse began to accelerate at a ridiculous rate. She swallowed, opened her eyes, and looked into a pair of twinkling brown ones. Kit opened her mouth, then closed it, unable to think of a thing to say.

Rafe grinned, his lips brushing lightly against her jaw line. He was sitting on the edge of the bed, his arms folded across his bare chest. "I figured it would be better to wake you rather than have you scream when this cold salve hits your skin." He pulled back the rust plaid sheets, eyeing the exposed length of her back. "It looks a lot better this morning."

Kit pulled herself together with great difficulty. It was evident from her surroundings that she had spent the night in the master bedroom. The next question was, where had the master spent the night? "You should have woken me. I could have gone back to the cottage." It was difficult to sound cool and detached under Rafe's caressing fingers.

"I did try," he admitted cheerfully, "but you were snoring too loudly." He playfully patted her curving derriere and slid off the bed, then stood looking down at her, her fiery hair splayed against the gold pillowcase, her sapphire-blue eyes wide and glowing in her sleep-flushed face. "Knowing what a stickler you are for convention, I went down to the cottage and brought back your jeans and a blouse. I'll keep Teresa and Matt occupied in the kitchen so you can come downstairs unnoticed."

Kit pushed herself up into a sitting position. Then, realizing her only attire was a pair of apricot nylon briefs, she hastily arranged the bed linen in a protective cover. A growing tension was building inside her. She watched Rafe slip into a light blue shirt and tuck the tails into matching trousers. She brushed back her hair, mustering her dignity. "Where did you sleep?" she asked lightly, trying to sound completely indifferent.

"In my bed. Right next to you," he stated baldly, his lips twisting into a wry smile at the angry flare of her nostrils. A charmed grin spread over his face, causing an instant tightening around her heart. "Had I intended to do more than just sleep next to you, I guarantee you would have known it." He picked up his tie and jacket, winked, and slipped out the door.

A shiver of pure physical awareness chased down Kit's spine. She drew in a swift breath at the subtle threat in his quietly spoken words, then stared at the closed door, attempting to analyze her feelings toward him. The ambivalence of her emotions showed plainly on her face. There was a sweet and sour reality about this whole situation.

Rafe was a devastatingly virile and attractive man, both physically and mentally. She was blantantly aware of the combustible mixture of their two chemistries. It was the first time in her life she had ever experienced such primitive sexual feelings toward a man—but that was all it was: one set of glands calling to another.

Kit's hands tangled roughly in her hair. They were totally incompatible, two people coming from different worlds. She had nothing to offer him. He was an out-of-reach star in another heaven. She had accepted the loneliness of her life, but she wasn't so foolish as to accept a casual affair with him as a substitute for something more permanent.

This is just a job, Kit reminded herself tautly. *You are here to play a part, and when it's over you will leave. And leave proud.* She was strong and tough and flexible, and she'd deal with the consequences of any more entanglements on a day-to-day basis.

CHAPTER SEVEN

"Advance token to the nearest railroad. If owned, pay owner twice the rental." Matt eyed the orange Chance card dispassionately, then moved his mounted cowboy to the B & O Railroad.

"Four hundred bucks," Kit demanded with a grin, holding out an eager palm.

He watched her double-check the colorful assortment of play money and handed his uncle the dice. "Mercenary thing. She just collected fifty bucks off of us on her Community Chest card."

Rafe laughed, threw the dice on the Monopoly board, and moved his racing car ten spaces, settling on Baltic Avenue. Matt handed him $200 for passing Go. Kit cleared her throat, smiled, and once again

132

held out her palm. "How much?" Rafe asked dryly, eyeing her happily flushed features.

"Baltic with a hotel is four hundred, sir." She batted her long dark lashes at him, shifting her position on the family room's fluffy shag rug to straighten out her white slacks and accept the rent.

"You're nickle-and-diming me to death, Kit." He sighed tolerantly, handing her an orange $500 bill from his towering collection of cash and receiving a blue fifty in change.

Kit moved her metal puppy nine from the Water Works, groaning audibly when her token landed on Rafe's Park Place.

"With a hotel, it's fifteen hundred, sweetheart," he said.

"I intend to get that all back," she warned sweetly. Circumspectly, she eyed Rafe's sinewy length, clad in a tan knit shirt and matching slacks.

There had been a subtle change in their relationship since the morning she had awoken in his bed. After an initial awkwardness, Kit had found herself growing more compliant to the situation, not viewing herself as a captive. It was, she acknowledged reasonably, due to a change of attitude on her part.

She had let herself become totally absorbed into the Morgan family unit. Teresa treated her like a daughter. Together they planned meals, cooked, and even cleaned. Matt had become the brother she had never had: teasing, arguing, and questioning. Rafe? Well, Rafe had become a friend rather than an enemy. A certain closeness had developed between them. Since he knew about her past, she had stopped feeling so angry and defensive; he, in turn, was more tolerant of her moods. The change was reflected in the lessening of tensions between them.

Kit had time to think, regenerate, and regain control of the situation. While she didn't like masquerading as Rafe's fiancée, she conceded that she had created the problem, and she was resolved to help him attain his goal: Tracy Shippley. In exchange, she was sharing and taking part in a real home—living each day, treasuring each moment, enjoying the most satisfying time of her life—until it came time for her to go.

The black-and-white dice clattered against the board, rolling a five. "Go directly to Jail," Matt grumbled, sliding his token onto the appropriate square.

Rafe landed on Oriental Avenue, and Kit regained a third of her losses. Her dice flipped into two definitive dots, sending her to Boardwalk.

"Looks like this does it, boys and girls," Rafe announced, grinning wolfishly and rubbing his hands together. "Two thousand dollars, and"—his long fingers pushed through Kit's stack of money—"I don't think you've got it."

"Take it easy, Simon Legree," Matt teased irreverently. "She can always mortgage."

"Actually," Kit said, smiling at both of them and studying her unpolished fingernails, "I've always believed in the Boy Scout motto: Be prepared." She reached into the scoop neck of her sleeveless, pink cabled sweater, extracted four orange bills, and handed them to Rafe. "From my private stock."

He tossed the paper aside and with one fluid movement had her pinned to the carpet with the full length of his rugged body. "Let's just see what else you're harboring in that vault," he drawled dangerously, his dark eyes twinkling devilishly.

Matt stopped laughing long enough to answer the telephone when it was apparent that neither of his opponents was going to acknowledge it.

Kit shrieked and madly clutched Rafe's arms, trying unsuccessfully to ward off his determined hands. "I never realized you were part octopus," she gasped, trying to wriggle out from under him.

His teeth flashed, and the grooves deepened in his laughing bronze face. "Stop fighting, sweetheart," he murmured, the hairs of his mustache scratching and teasing her swelling cleavage.

Kit's palms flattened against his hard, unyielding chest, her fingers tangling in the thick mat of dark hair curling out from the open neck of his gold shirt. It was a struggle to ignore the warm, intoxicating glow that was spreading over her skin under the intimate entanglement of their bodies.

Matt cleared his throat loudly, causing both Rafe and Kit to turn their heads. "That was Jack Shippley," he announced in his best voice of doom, both dark eyes focusing on Kit's rapidly fading smile.

"We're all invited to a barbecue tomorrow. Tracy and Miss LaDonna are home."

Kit turned her head, her pliant figure stiffening at the news. "It looks like the game's afoot for real," she said in a low voice, her eyes locking into those of the man above her.

The Shippley women resembled a trio of dainty petit fours: Mama, LaDonna, in lemon yellow; Marybeth in dainty pink; and Tracy in mint green. Three tiny, delicate creatures who were born to be taken care of, Kit conceded ruefully, feeling more self-conscious than usual about her own Amazonian build.

The last time she had visited the Shippley ranch was as an employee enjoying her boss's Labor Day picnic feast. Then she had admired the rolling expanse of lawns and gardens that surrounded the Georgian-style house, which looked as if it had been plucked from the pages of *Gone with the Wind.* Today, the grounds looked too manicured and artificial, the massive white house too immaculate and unblemished, and despite the unblinking heat of the sun, there seemed to be a definite arctic air mass blowing in her direction.

"I think I've been dealt the losing hand," she muttered, slowing her long-legged stride to a standstill.

Rafe stopped, his gaze studying her set features. "Don't tell me you're throwing your cards in already," he remarked coolly. Two strong hands settled on either side of her waist, ready to halt any attempt at flight.

Kit looked up into his dark, brooding gaze and smiled sweetly. "Three blond queens take a lone redhead in any poker game."

A slow grin spread across his rugged features, his brow lifting in amusement. "That all depends on how well stacked the redhead is. You've never let me down before."

"Just remember, I'm not the type to think everything said with a Southern drawl is cute," she warned lightly, her fingers plucking an infinitesimal thread off the alligator on the pocket of his pristine white knit shirt before coming around to smooth out an unwrinkled collar. It was a very territorial gesture that she instinctively knew would not go unnoticed.

"I have absolutely no worries that you can handle yourself in any situation," Rafe countered smoothly. His fingers deftly untied, then retied the already perfect bow on the shoestring straps of her black, daisy-strewn sun dress. He slid a sinewy arm around her waist and guided her across the lawn.

"Afternoon, ladies," he drawled, politely tipping the brim of his black Stetson. "Miss LaDonna, Tracy, I don't believe you've had the pleasure of meeting my fiancée."

Kit's blue eyes sparkled with amusement; she sincerely doubted this was a pleasure for any of them. She graciously extended her hand to Mrs. Shippley. The elder woman limply grasped her fingertips. The

137

barely perceptible acknowledgment of her existence by both Tracy and Marybeth compelled Kit to respond in kind, with a regal nod of her own. She felt the comforting strength of Rafe's hand spread across the base of her spine.

"Where is that darlin' nephew of yours?" LaDonna Shippley smiled brilliantly up at Rafe.

"I'm afraid Matt had a previous engagement this afternoon," he returned amiably. "I trust you had an enjoyable trip back east."

"Enjoyable but expensive for Jack." She laughed loudly, her heavily ringed fingers tidying an errant strand of hair that grazed her temple. "When is your mama comin' home?"

Kit's ears stayed with the conversation, but her eyes surreptitiously strayed to Tracy Shippley. She was a few years older than Marybeth and, if possible, even thinner. Her platinum hair shimmered like silver under the sun, falling to her slender shoulders in perfectly controlled waves. Her features were delicate, yet finely defined. So far she hadn't uttered a word, but her hungry green gaze spoke volumes, devouring every inch of Rafe Morgan. Kit had little doubt Tracy would abandon her efforts to reclaim her strayed man.

At the sound of her name, Kit turned and saw the Stanfords heading in her direction. She waved and smiled eagerly in response to their greeting. With Rafe in tow, she gravitated toward them as if they were a lifeline. The two men wandered off in search of tall, frosted mugs of icy cold Coors, leaving their female companions to settle at one of the red-and-white-gingham-covered tables.

"I was just telling Jim that if two people ever needed to be rescued, it was you and Rafe," Gretchen Stanford said, blowing dust off the lenses of her aviator sunglasses.

Kit turned, visibly startled by her statement. "Rescued?" she asked cautiously, her blue eyes riveted on the tall brunette's animated face.

"From the three blond dwarfs," Gretched cracked dryly, her mouth spreading into a wide, unrepentant grin. "They ignore me, too. It has to do with my father." At Kit's puzzled frown, she laughed and explained. "He had the audacity to raise sheep in the middle of all these cattlemen."

"Doesn't their attitude bother you?"

Gretchen shook back her long dark hair. "The only person they're hurting is themselves. I make a wonderful friend," she said with such mock affectation that Kit couldn't help but laugh. "I think it's a terrible waste of time to dwell on the past. But the Shippleys are one of those peculiar breed of folk who think that impeccable lineage makes the only acceptable acquaintances."

Kit felt a sharp pain knife through her heart. Gretchen Stanford knew about her background! She wondered how many others did. "And you don't feel that way?" she inquired slowly, the words oddly strained as they pushed past the hard lump in her throat.

"No, I don't, and neither do most of the people you'll meet here. Remember, the bulk of the settlers who came west were rough, tough pioneers. A lot of them ended swinging from trees, condemned as rustlers and outlaws. I would imagine even the Shippleys have a skeleton rattling in a closet somewhere."

"Why do you accept their invitations?"

"For Jim," Gretchen replied, her gaze straying to her tall husband at the bar. "He has to deal with Jack in his business, and I try not to let my feelings get in the way. Besides," she added with a broad grin, her hand patting Kit's arm, "I'd break bread with the devil himself as long as he did the cooking and the cleaning up."

Kit smiled at Gretchen's sincere offer of friendship. Her bleak eyes shifted to the large group of laughing, chattering people assembled on the lawn. She wondered how many of them would feel the same way. Old sins take a long time to die, she reflected, especially within one's self.

"I don't know about you girls, but we're starving." Jim Stanford's deep voice cut through Kit's meditation. The four of them headed for the main buffet table.

The Shippleys spared no expense when it came to putting on a barbecue. Massive tables groaned under the weight of tons of cold salads, bean dishes, onions, pickles, coleslaw, jalapeño peppers and rice, a black kettle full of rich chili, and the most tender roasted quail, beef, and lamb. Gretchen had whispered that they were, indeed, putting on the dog by using china and silverware rather than the usual disposables.

All the down-home friendly smiles and the wealth of warm greetings Kit had received during the barbecue paled into insignificance at the sound of Tracy Shippley's perfectly cultured voice. "I thought Rafe would pick up something on the cruise, but penicillin usual takes care of that little problem."

Kit continued to fill two delicate china cups from a massive silver coffee urn, her face and body under rigid self-control. "I didn't realize you were such an expert on social diseases, Tracy." She placed the filled cups on the pristine white tablecloth and turned to face her tiny adversary. She was grateful the confrontation was here, in a far corner away from the main crowd. She had the feeling it was not going to be pleasant.

Tracy's cat eyes narrowed. Her small fingers twisted the sash of her delicate sun dress. "I imagine you would know more about that than I, being your mother's daughter." She smiled maliciously, her small chin rising in silent challenge.

Kit leaned her hip against the table, cocked her copper head, and eyed the platinum-haired sophisticate with tolerant amusement. "I see you really haven't progressed much beyond your days of black-balling rival sorority sisters at college. No wonder it was so easy for me to attract Rafe."

"You bitch!" Tracy spat viciously, her tiny hand moving to strike. The motion was suddenly halted when Kit intimidatingly straightened her tall body. Tracy smiled, her tongue running slowly over perfect, pearl-white teeth, her green eyes dropping to Kit's left hand. "There is still no ring, and I know for a fact he hasn't taken you anyplace off the ranch," she observed slyly.

"Rafe will take me anywhere I want to go," Kit replied confidently.

One finely plucked brow arched. "See if he'll take you to the dinner dance at the club tonight," Tracy tossed off casually before sliding away to rejoin her other guests.

Kit reached over and picked up the coffee cups, wryly noting the slight clatter her trembling fingers caused the delicate porcelain dishes. She should have been amused at the whole situation; it was the first time she had ever been considered a rival for any man's affections. Instead, she felt sickened at the other woman's vengeance in obtaining her objective of possessing Rafe Morgan.

A large hand settled on her shoulder. She knew whose it was. "Your plan is working perfectly," Kit said with deceptive calm. "By tonight you should have Tracy eating out of your hand." She turned, expecting to find a self-satisfied grin. Instead Rafe's dark gaze broodingly studied her restrained features.

The elegant chandeliered dining room of the River

Run Golf and Country Club stood waiting to cater to every whim of the prestigious crowd. The women were dazzling in couturier creations and sparkling jewels, and the men resplendent in white evening wear punctuated with dark bow ties.

Kit nervously fingered the soft folds of her long gown. It was not a designer original, but the one-shouldered style suited her tall figure. The sheer material of the dress was laced with dusty hues of color. She had arranged her hair in a mass of fiery curls. Her makeup was soft and inviting and her only jewels were pearl studs in her ears. Not quite as grand as the others, but for the evening Kit had become Cinderella.

Her gaze slid to Rafe, who stood by her side, tall and commanding in an impeccably tailored white evening jacket over dark trousers. Together they towered over almost every other couple in the room.

When she had first mentioned the dinner dance that afternoon, Kit hadn't failed to notice the bored expression that had settled on Rafe's rugged features. She had the oddest feeling that he had consented to attend only out of deference to her, which was silly, because the only reason she wanted to go was to help him!

Rafe had said little during the short drive to the club; now he appeared faultlessly courteous and attentive, acting for all the world like a devoted fiancé. As they mingled with the crowd, Kit spied Tracy Shippley clinging tightly to the arm of a handsome man whose eyes watched her every move. The tiny blonde looked positively awe-inspiring in a bare-shouldered gown, the lilac material draping in shirred columns around her perfect figure.

Some sixth sense told Kit that tonight would be the climax to her performance as Rafe's fiancée. She was determined to enjoy the enchantment to the fullest, knowing it would never come again.

The evening was an unqualified success. The combination of superb gourmet food and wine, the constant attention from her handsome escort, and the entertaining conversation of their tablemates succeeded in convincing Kit that she had, indeed, stepped into a fairy tale.

Rafe proved more than an adequate partner on the dance floor; their bodies moved in fluid unison to the throbbing beat of the music, which varied from romantic rhythms to an occasional lapse into Willie Nelson and the Bee Gees.

Kit was flexing her slightly aching feet when Tracy Shippley slid into Rafe's unoccupied chair next to her. "I must admit I was surprised to see you here tonight," she said, her voice clipped and brittle.

"I believe I told you this afternoon that Rafe takes me wherever I want to go," Kit returned quietly, settling back against the upholstered chair. Outwardly she appeared relaxed and confident; inside every nerve and muscle was coiled like a spring under tension.

Tracy fingered the magnificent amethyst pendant

that encircled her slim neck, her green eyes throwing a malicious gaze in the redhead's direction. "You latched on to him during one of our on-again, off-again periods, but I saw him watching me tonight. He was jealous that I was here with someone else."

Kit smiled, her gaze shifting to easily find Rafe's tall figure at the bar. "I think that's wishful thinking on your part. He didn't even notice you were here."

Tracy's voice was almost hysterical with fury, and Kit was thankful their dinner companions were enjoying the dance music. "You can only ride high so long before someone slips a burr under your saddle."

"I'm a very skilled rider," Kit replied, leaning forward, her tone calm and positive, "and you are such an insignificant burr."

A strangled sound escaped from Tracy's throat. She jumped off the chair and flounced back across the dance floor into the waiting arms of her brown-haired companion.

It was prophetic, Kit decided, eyeing the ornate wall clock, that its hands had just registered midnight. In fairy tales the heroine's happiness always came to a crashing end at the witching hour. She stood, proud and tall, when Rafe returned to the table. "I'd like to leave now," she told him quietly.

His dark head tilted sideways, scrutinizing her unusually expressive features. "I haven't finished my brandy," he said.

Kit smiled sweetly, reached out, and plucked the balloon-shaped snifter from his fingers. She drained the amber-colored liquid in three gulps, her eyes watering when the fiery liquor hit her stomach. "You have now," she countered hoarsely, her eyes blinking furiously. She turned and walked to the main doors, leaving an amused Rafe to follow.

Kit sat stiffly erect in the bucket seat of the Porsche, her eyes vainly trying to focus on the swiftly passing scenery. "Actually, the more I think about it, the more I'm convinced you couldn't find anyone better than Tracy," she told Rafe. "She's breathtakingly beautiful, her education is impeccable, and she simply shines at any social function. She's charming."

"That's the tenth time you've called her charming, and each time it sounds like a four-letter word."

She pointedly ignored Rafe's amused chuckle, struggling against a growing feeling of lassitude resulting from her hastily downing his brandy. "No, really. Tracy will make you a perfect wife. She knows all about ranching and will be an invaluable asset in your business. What more could you ask for?" Kit's thick voice demanded almost belligerently. "When you marry her, you're halfway to having the perfect American family. You already have the required station wagon and dog. All that's left is the one point eight children. But don't worry," she assured him quickly, "I'm sure she can buy the kids from the Neiman-Marcus catalog so she won't lose her eighteen-inch waist."

"Your claws are showing, Kitten."

She turned in her seat, her eyes wide and innocent as they focused on Rafe's grinning profile. "Just because Tracy gives me a headache does not mean she isn't . . ."

"Charming," he supplied dryly. "I think the brandy is talking."

Kit clamped her mouth shut, slid lower in the plush seat, and glared resentfully out the windshield. She couldn't entirely blame the brandy for loosening her tongue. Everything she said about Tracy was true, and it seemed pointless to keep denying it.

Rafe parked the sports car next to the cottage and indulgently helped her from the front seat. "I have shoes higher off the ground than this car," she grumbled, struggling out of the Porsche with little grace. "Why didn't you use the Mercedes?"

"I didn't want to be in the position of being used as a taxi service" was his insouciant reply as he held open the front door.

Nosey gave them a boisterous greeting. Kit knelt down, praising his efforts as a watchdog, then favoring him with a rawhide chew stick she had left on the end table. The dog danced excitedly, then raced into a far corner to happily gnaw his reward.

"Mind if I have that brandy now?" Rafe inquired, turning toward the small chrome and glass liquor cart.

"My house is your house," Kit cracked sweetly, switching on the table lamp to low and settling herself on the sofa.

147

"God, it's hot in here," he breathed, putting his glass down to remove his jacket and tie. "You are allowed to use the air conditioner."

"I can stand the heat," she retorted perversely, uncomfortably aware of the fact that Rafe had also unbuttoned his pleated dress shirt nearly to the waist. The mat of dark hair on his bronze chest seemed to cause an unusual curling sensation in her stomach. Kit lowered her eyes, her fingers busily unbuckling her beige evening sandals. "Things worked out perfectly, in any case," she said, easing her tired feet from the shoes.

"What?" Rafe looked and sounded confused. He walked over to stand in front of her.

"Tracy was really upset. She's ready to come back on any terms." Kit wriggled her feet in the plush pile carpet.

"Did it ever occur to you that I like things just the way they are?" Rafe asked.

Kit's eyes flew open. She pushed herself off the couch and stared at him. "What's the matter with you?" she demanded furiously. "This is exactly what you wanted, what you've been waiting for. How much crawling do you want that poor girl to do?"

His jaw dropped. "You're worried about her?"

"I'm worried about all of us." Her gaze collided with his and wavered nervously at the raw emotion she saw there. She took a deep controlling breath. "It seems to me you're getting some perverse pleasure out of manipulating the both of us. How much God-like devotion do you want?" she spat out, her voice loaded with contempt. "I thought you were someone special, someone who really cared about people. But you're not. You're as ruthless and cruel as they come."

"In that case," he growled savagely, slamming his glass down on the end table, his leg thrusting aside the octagonal coffee table, "you won't mind if I live up to your expectations."

Rafe's hands clamped viselike on either side of her waist, yanking her roughly against him. His mouth cruelly swallowed her strangled protest, his hard tongue raping her lips, forcing them apart for his exploration.

Her palms slammed hard against his shoulders in a valiant attempt to break free. He merely imprisoned her wrists with his large hands, propelling her backward onto the sofa so that he was half on top of her, pinning her against the cushions with his superior strength.

His mouth never left hers, lustily devouring the life-giving oxygen, making her dizzy and light-headed. Despite her struggles, her body traitorously responded to his rough caresses.

"Don't fight me, Kit," Rafe muttered hoarsely, his lips rubbing against the creamy jasmine-scented skin of her throat.

"Stop, please," she begged weakly, but her freed hands sought his shoulders, and her fingers clutched the sinewy warm flesh instead of pushing it away. "You don't know what you're doing."

"I know exactly what I'm doing," he growled. His hands tangled in her silken mane, scattering a shower of hairpins and unleashing the flame-colored curls. His dark head burrowed against the curve of her neck, his capable fingers quickly disposing of the clasp that held her dress at the shoulder. "I want you, Kit," he said, pushing aside the soft folds of the material, his hands cupping her full breast possessively, his velvety dark eyes glittering with raw desire into her luminous blue orbs. "I'll make you want me."

His mouth was wonderfully warm and passionately persuasive when it again closed tenderly over her bruised lips. His hands stroked her trembling body, quelling the initial panic and fear that had been sparked by his anger.

His kisses and caresses, more potent than the brandy she had consumed, sapped her strength and reduced her resistance until she was aching with desire, moaning with intense arousal. She had been starving for years, hungry for love, waiting to be wanted. Rafe was giving her a taste of what she had been denied and she eagerly reached for it.

Her fingers threaded in the vibrant dark hair at the nape of his neck, she pressed his head tightly against her breast, shivering at the touch of his warm lips and the moist hard tongue that curled around her taut nipple.

His breathing was ragged. He shifted his weight, his hands boldly pushing up the skirt of her gown, seeking the sensitive skin of her inner thighs. His thumb and forefinger gently teased the thrusting peaks of her flushed breasts. His mouth moved to rain kisses over her face.

"I'll take care of you," he promised huskily. "I can give you everything you'll ever want." His virile fingers boldly ruptured the sheer weave of her panty hose, seeking the leg opening of her nylon briefs.

It would be so easy to step over the edge of sanity and end her innocence, but her ruling passion dissolved under her mind's conquering whispers of reason.

She was mistaking sex for love. Rafe was willing to give her things in exchange for her body. She had always condemned her mother for taking money and gifts from men. Wouldn't she be doing the same thing?

Kit froze, her body no longer pliant and submissive. "Stop it, Rafe. I don't want you." Her voice sounded strong, resistance replacing desire with each passing second.

Something in her tone must have communicated itself to Nosey. The silver schnauzer lunged from his dog bed, growling deep in his throat.

Rafe shook his head, amazed at the sudden turn of events. Kit used his confusion to her advantage, scrambling out of his embrace to the safety of her feet. Her trembling fingers hastily refastened the shoulder clasp of her dress. "Please leave. Just go," she ordered, her skin still tingling with arousal.

Slowly Rafe got to his feet, his chest heaving under his rough breathing. "Kit, I—"

"Get out! Just get out!" she demanded angrily, still refusing to look at him. Another low growl came from the dog, who now stood guard at her side; then she heard the slam of the door.

CHAPTER EIGHT

Kit rubbed the tension in her forehead with numb fingers. Her eyes focused on the collection of suitcases and clothes that littered her mattress. She had packed and unpacked at least twenty times, finally settling on what looked like an oversized handbag that would hold her essentials. She zipped the beige canvas carry-all shut, hugging it tightly against her breast, hoping it would quiet her madly pounding heart.

"It's the best thing for everyone," she told Nosey. The silver schnauzer cocked his head, his normally floppy ears stiff with attention, alert to her every move. She smiled at him, dropped onto the edge of the bed, and massaged his strong neck. The dog had never left her side all night. Six feet had worn a path through the pale blue carpet, while her chaotic emotions had tried to make sense out of the events of that evening.

Once again, Kit asserted ruefully, she had precipitated the entire chain of events. On the drive home from the country club she had continually brought up Tracy's name, never realizing just how upset Rafe must have been at seeing her with another man. She had goaded him with words, until his heightened anger and frustrations had erupted into an unthinking act that had sexually aroused both of them.

Both of them. Kit stood up and ran a weary hand through her hair. She, too, had been pulled into the vortex of physical desire. She had never been loved, never felt love, never received love. All her life she had dreamed of being loved and last night, for one brief moment, she had almost had her desire fulfilled.

But this man was not for her. She didn't love Rafe. She had been using him. She had stayed here too long and taken too much, enjoying the homey, relaxed atmosphere at the ranch and sharing in a family unit for the first time. She had played her part well enough to sufficiently ignite Tracy Shippley's wrath. It would only be a matter of time before the woman capitulated to Rafe's demands.

Although there was a strong attraction between Rafe and her, Kit knew she could give him nothing —nothing but her body, and it was foolish to think that sex would bind them together in some magical, mysterious way. If she stayed here any longer, she would only become a major source of trouble.

The intercom buzzed through the quiet cottage. Kit smoothed her hair and picked up the receiver. Rafe's voice was brusque and sharp in her ear. "I need you at the house. Ted's here. It's about the clinic." The line went dead before she could reply.

Kit made a quick stop to apologize to Teresa for missing her usually delicious Sunday brunch, giving the wiry housekeeper an affectionate hug to relieve the concern that plainly showed on her angular face.

In the study she found Rafe and Ted Vail poring over the files on the clinic project. Kit wiped suddenly clammy hands along the sides of her sand-colored linen dress and cleared her throat, concentrating her gaze on the young lawyer's ruddy features.

"Come in and sit down, Kit," Rafe ordered, not lifting his own dark eyes from the stack of papers scattered on top of the wide oak desk. "Tell her our problem, Ted."

"I honestly didn't expect to ruin everyone's Sunday," Ted sighed, running a hand through his close-cropped blond hair. "Last night Ginny and I were at the lawyers' club. It was one of those chicken-à-la-king functions." He grimaced wryly, flopping into the chair across from Kit. "Anyway, I ran into Ben Hammner, the lawyer who's handling the land transfer to the clinic from K. C. Whittier. Ben had a few too many and let it slip that Rafe was going to have to pay big bucks if he wanted the land, now that George Olson, Whittier's nephew, was running the company."

Kit's smooth forehead puckered with concentration, her gaze shifting for a moment to study Rafe's granite-hard features. "I didn't realize that K.C. had lost control of his company," she said slowly. "I just talked to Phyllis Vogel, his secretary, on Wednesday. She said the papers were on her boss's desk and Jim Stanford could start warming up his bulldozers."

"I've been expecting those papers every day myself," Ted admitted. "Every time I checked with Hammner's office, they'd tell me the delay was down at the recording clerk's office." He looked apologetically toward his boss. "I had no idea Olson was easing Whittier out. It has to be the smoothest, quietest takeover on record."

"That's what bothers me," Rafe countered thoughtfully. "It's too damn quiet." His dark eyes shifted to Kit. She looked crisp and cool, completely untouchable. A muscle twitched in his cheek, and his voice came out harsher than he intended. "I'm surprised Phyllis didn't call you about this news."

Kit turned calmly, not a flicker of emotion crossing her face. "I'm surprised too. May I?" She pointed to the telephone.

Phyllis Vogel answered in the middle of the second ring, her voice light and bubbly in reply to Kit's greeting. "This is wonderful. I hope you're going to tell me you're coming to visit. We housebound patients always need cheering up."

"You sound pretty cheerful to me," Kit returned easily. "What are you recovering from?"

"My old nemesis, phlebitis," Phyllis explained, her voice suddenly losing its brightness. "The damn leg is swollen and painful. My doctor tells me I've got until Tuesday to improve or it's into the hospital. My sister is playing nurse."

"I'm really sorry, Phyl. When we talked last week—"

"Well, I was trying to get everything tidied up for K.C.," she interrupted. "He was rushing off to Mexico to join some archaeological dig."

"So that's why George Olson is running the company."

"George!" Phyllis laughed. "That dimwit can't sharpen a pencil, let alone run a company. No, K.C. has special people he leaves in charge. That's why I didn't hesitate to take time off. Actually, when he's gone there's very little that needs to be done in my office."

Kit shook her head, trying to assimilate this news. "Phyl, I'm going to switch you to a conference speaker. I think Rafe and Ted Vail have something to tell you."

"Say, what's going on?" The secretary's voice became increasingly alarmed.

"Phyllis, this is Rafe. We just learned that George Olson is trying to take over K.C.'s company."

"What!"

Ted Vail hastily told her of his conversation with Ben Hammner over the change on the clinic project. There was a stunned silence on the line.

"Something is very wrong," said Phyllis. "Let me make a few phone calls. I'll get back to you shortly." There was no ignoring the grim determination in her voice.

After forty minutes of watching Rafe prowl around the study like a caged lion and listening to Ted clatter his spoon against the sides of his coffee mug, Kit thought she'd scream. Luckily, the phone did it for her. She tossed aside the paper clips she had been rearranging and scooped up the receiver, simultaneously punching the speaker button. "Phyl?"

"Yup, it's me. Are you all listening?" At the sound of three varied affirmatives, Phyllis laughed. "Well, I guess I have to give the devil his due. Nephew Georgy is much smarter than anyone ever anticipated. The cagey bastard sent out letters to all the stockholders offering them bigger profits, quick action on new ventures, and a more youthful performance in management if they would sign their proxies over to him. He must have been planning this for a long time, but threw the ball in motion on Thursday, taking advantage of me being out and K.C. being a thousand miles away. He's got a stockholders' meeting set for Tuesday."

"How did you learn all this?" Kit marveled, completely in awe of the woman's business prowess.

"I may be physically disabled, honey, but I can still pinch a few nerves and make people jump," Phyllis told her dryly. "The immediate problem is getting K.C. back here to fight. He won't have any trouble winning once he's here to pull his own strings. Rafe, you won't have to worry about paying for that land."

"The land was the least of my worries," Rafe told her bluntly, settling his tall frame in a chair behind his desk. "I don't like seeing someone railroaded out of a business they sweated and nurtured like a child. How can I help?"

"I was hoping you'd ask that," Phyllis said, her voice breaking in relief. "You've been to K.C.'s place in Mexico, haven't you?"

"Last fall. It's quite a ways off the beaten track."

"That's right," Phyllis agreed. "No phones, no shortwave, no radio, no TV. Nothing but the steamy jungle and its beasties and a few Mayan ruins. If I could, I'd hop on a plane and—"

"You can't," Rafe interrupted briskly. "But I can." He looked at his watch and rubbed his hand across his jaw. "I can get him back here by noon tomorrow."

"That's enough time. I'll have a few trusted people working around the clock on this end. We won't have any problem facing the stockholders on Tuesday." She gave a light laugh. "You've got yourself a good man there, Kit."

Kit's blue eyes collided with Rafe's dark somber

ones, her cheeks staining under his cynical stare. She swallowed. "I guess you're right."

"Rafe," Phyllis continued, "can you stop at my place on your way to the airport? I have a few things being sent over that K.C. will need to see."

"Kit and I will be there within the hour," Rafe promised and slid the receiver back onto the phone. "How long will it take you to throw a few things in a suitcase?" he asked Kit, ignoring her surprised look.

"I'm already packed."

He sighed heavily. "I thought you might be."

Less than two hours later, Kit found herself walking through the airport parking lot carrying her beige carry-all and an unfamiliar leather attaché case. Twenty-four hours ago she had made up her mind to leave, never expecting to be doing just that—but with Rafe Morgan by her side.

They had made a brief stop at Phyllis's midtown apartment to pick up papers and more definitive directions to K.C.'s jungle hideaway. They had left the slim, gray-haired secretary in high spirits, despite the painful blood clot in her leg.

Kit nervously eyed the outdoor video display of plane arrivals and departures. "Which flight do we have tickets for?"

"We won't be needing any tickets," Rafe informed her, directing her away from the main terminal building toward a small hangar and a fleet of private aircraft. She stopped and looked at him, her eyes wide with an unspoken question. He grinned and pointed toward a cream twin-engine Lear jet that two mechanics were crawling over. "I'm playing pilot. In less than two hours we'll land at Villahermosa and check in with customs and immigration; then it's by jeep inland. I'm glad you wore something sensible," he added dryly, eyeing her white cotton blouse, tan slacks, and rubber-soled desert boots.

Cautiously, Kit mounted the small set of stairs that led into the plane. She followed Rafe's instructions, ignoring the sumptuous passenger seats to settle in the copilot's chair in the tiny cockpit. Rafe slid easily into the pilot's chair, looped a set of headphones on, and began a seemingly one-sided conversation with the control tower.

Kit tried to act nonchalant as she buckled her seat belt. In truth, she was a nervous wreck. She had never been in any type of aircraft before, and the small cabin was beginning to make her feel claustrophobic.

When the plane began to taxi down the runway, she closed her eyes tightly, blotting out the millions of dials and gauges on the control panel and the scenery that rushed madly past the tiny windows. A horrible pressure in her ears forced her body down in the brown velvet cushions. Her head felt about to explode.

Rafe's hand nudged her arm. She opened her eyes and looked at a package of gum. "This will help," he said softly. "Why didn't you tell me you'd never flown before?"

"It's that noticeable?" she asked.

His teeth flashed in an understanding grin. "Your hyperventilating gave you away."

Kit slid a stick of gum into her mouth and began chewing. She sighed gratefully when her ears pooped. "I guess I'm not the world traveler type. I was seasick and now airsick." At Rafe's hastily raised brow, she gave him a weak smile. "Don't worry, I won't be sick all over your dials."

"Just relax," Rafe instructed, his voice low and comforting. "If you'd like, I can tell you exactly what I'm doing."

"That's all right," she said quickly, furiously chewing her gum. "Just make sure we don't run into anything." She concentrated on trying to calm her pounding heart and finding enough air to fill her lungs. She had heard Rafe say they were at 30,000 feet, and looking out, she believed it. There was not a speck of land in sight. Below them billowed a collection of frothy white clouds etched in sunlight. Around and above them stretched an incredible expanse of blue sky.

Kit had to admit that the interior of the cockpit was as quiet as the front seat of the Mercedes and the flight just as smooth. She took another deep breath of cool, recycled air. Rafe seemed as proficient a pilot as he was a driver, and that thought relaxed her further.

"I think we have a few things that need talking out."

Rafe's bald statement caused the gum to disintegrate in Kit's mouth. She shifted uncomfortably in her seat, another tight band of anxiety forming across her chest.

"About last night. I'd like to apologize. I—"

"I should be the one to apologize," Kit interrupted, her eyes on the green sweep lines of the radarscope.

"What!"

"Listen," she sighed and turned toward him. "I know what a major annoyance I was last night. I should have seen how upset you were about Tracy being with another man. I kept goading you and I said things about you that I didn't mean." She placed her hand on his arm, giving him a comforting squeeze. "I know how frustrated you must be. But once we get back, I'm positive everything will work out between the two of you." Kit smiled confidently into his dumbstruck brown eyes. She was glad for the chance to end the animosity that had invaded their friendship.

Rafe just continued to stare at her, an intense, searching stare that gradually caused her smile to fade. He shook his head, muttered something she didn't catch, then went back to talking on the radio.

Kit shrugged and settled back into her seat, unwrapping another stick of peppermint gum. By the time they crossed the Tropic of Cancer, she had chewed the entire pack.

The twenty-mile drive from Villahermosa was quite pleasant. The landscape that followed the curved, twisted highway gave the illusion of a gray-green prickly carpet. Massive rows of agave plants blanketed the terrain. Henequen, the yellow fiber obtained from their swordlike, razor-sharp leaves, was used to make rope. Intermingled with the agave plants were what appeared to be overgrown pineapples, but Rafe told her they were tequilana plants, the juices of which yielded the fiery, potent tequila the country was famous for.

Then suddenly the sunlight, the gentle breezes, and the smooth highway were gone, replaced by a hacked-out road in a dark, steamy forest. Little sun penetrated the sweltering shade of this dense canopy of tropical vegetation. Thick vines tangled around mango and banana trees. Brilliant poincianas brightened the greenness with vibrant splashes of red.

The air was no longer clean and fresh but thick with the rank smell of decay from fallen limbs and trees rotting in the moist undergrowth. In a matter of minutes, Kit's eyes blurred from sweat. She eased her clammy blouse from her skin, feeling the perspiration run in rivulets down her back. Hordes of mosquitoes and black flies swarmed around their heads.

Rafe was busy fighting with the steering wheel, maneuvering the jeep over the rutted, muddy jungle track. It was a teeth-rattling ride of hard, jarring sensations that pounded the spine.

"This is the forest primeval—standing like the Druids of old." Henry Wadsworth Longfellow's poem echoed through Kit's mind, and the description seemed most fitting. It wasn't hard to imagine the mysterious culture of the Maya flourishing here, Kit thought, a cold shudder coursing down her aching, perspiring spine. The primitive forest seemed the perfect setting for grisly ancient rituals presided over by evil, leering jaguars and stone demons. And yet, from such an unholy setting the Indians achieved a brilliance in architecture and astronomy that rivaled today's scientific achievements.

A massive stone house loomed out of the clearing. Rafe slid the jeep to a welcome stop next to the thatched-roofed veranda. "I feel like I've just ridden the meanest bronc this side of the Rio Grande," he said, his fingers still gripping the steering wheel.

"It was never like this in all those Tarzan movies I watched," Kit agreed. It took a few minutes before either of them was able to climb out of the jeep and negotiate terra firma.

Kit followed Rafe up three stone steps. He knocked, waited, and then opened the front door. Together they walked into the quiet house. Kit was surprised by the open, spacious interior. The massive living-dining area was filled with attractive hand-made furniture with woven hemp seats. The kitchen was unusually modern, with a gas stove, sink, and refrigerator. There was a bathroom with modern fixtures. Somehow, she had expected an outhouse with a half-moon carved in the door. Large ceiling fans created a cool breeze. Rafe explained that the power came from a hydroelectric generator at a nearby waterfall.

"Well," he announced, after inspecting the house thoroughly, "it appears that no one has been here for a couple of days. I'd guess that K.C. is staying at the Mayan dig site."

"That means we continue our safari," Kit returned unenthusiastically, her gaze wandering to the view of the thick jungle.

"That means I continue the safari," he countered, striding over to the knapsack he'd brought in. "It shouldn't take me long to find the dig using the map Phyllis made and following the jungle path. You can wait here, just in case he comes back."

"But Tarzan always took Jane. He'd never leave her alone. I—" She stopped, gasping as Rafe buckled on a holster and checked the cylinder of his revolver. "What's . . . what's that for?"

"Just in case I run into something that wants me for lunch," he returned dryly. He turned, hands on his slim jean-covered hips, and eyed her patiently. "Listen, I'm perfectly willing to let you play liberated lady. I'll let you lead the safari through the tick-infested vegetation. I'll even let you be the first one to step on the fire ant hills and—"

"All right, all right," she capitulated ruefully.

"You've made your point. How long do you think you're going to be gone?" She looked worried.

Rafe walked over, caught her chin in his long fingers, and turned her somber face up to his. "I'll be back as fast as I can. It gets dark early and it's the rainy season." His lips touched her damp forehead. "Just relax. I'll leave you the flare gun. Just aim it up and pull the trigger. In the meantime, don't leave the house, don't drink the water, and keep an eye out for scorpions."

"In other words, have a good time," she returned lightly and received a playful slap on her posterior. Uneasily, Kit watched the thick, twisted vegetation gobble up Rafe's tall figure. She stayed on the porch listening to the sounds of the jungle. Myriad birds and parrots chattered their complaints under the canopy of tangled vines. An odd wail pierced the air, sending a chill over her clammy flesh. Everything went deathly quiet. "It's only a monkey," Kit told herself out loud. Her blue eyes darted around the area. A rustling sound and movement in some near-by bushes caused her to back into the house and securely close the door.

After a marathon session of slapping and swatting, Kit gave up trying to control the mosquitoes and flies. It was apparent the screened windows gave the annoying insects little trouble in reaching a tasty target.

K.C. Whittier had an impressive collection of archaeology books scattered on the dining room table. In an attempt to ward off paranoia, Kit began reading and was transported into the seventh-century world of the Maya.

Numerous photos and drawings showed her the nearby ruins of Palenque and its fabled palace, home of the ruler Pacal, which towered above the ancient city. Palenque became sacred as the westernmost city of the Maya. Here hillside mausoleums brought to mind the startling similarities to Egypt's Valley of the Kings.

A polite cough sounded from the kitchen, abruptly returning Kit to the twentieth century. There, framed in the alcove, stood an Indian. A large hand-woven straw hat shaded his face. He was dressed in a white cotton shirt and trousers and a colorful tunic with unique tribal markings woven into the fabric. On his feet were the traditional Mexican huarache sandals, and a bright red kerchief encircled the tanned column of his throat. He moved into the room with awkward efficiency, setting a wriggling white bag on the floor.

Kit stood up and smiled hesitantly, wishing she could see more of his face. She hoped he spoke English. Her knowledge of Spanish was extremely rudimentary and her knowledge of Indian dialects nil.

Bronzed fingers removed the straw hat, revealing a face that was lean and simple, not characteristically Indian at all. A thick crop of gray hair matched the stubble of beard on his tanned features. A pair of light blue eyes studied her. A smile broke across his face. "You certainly would have caused a commotion among the Maya with that hair and height."

"K.C. Whittier?" Kit asked hopefully, studying the firm face and lean body that belied the fact that he was in his late sixties.

He nodded. "I know who you are. Kit Forrester. Right? Phyllis's description matches you perfectly." Grinning, K.C. walked over and shook her hand. "What the devil are you doing here?"

Kit opened her mouth, sighed, then closed it. There didn't seem any easy way to tell him the facts. "Rafe Morgan and I flew down to bring you back to San Antonio. Your nephew is pulling together proxies to take control of your company."

"The devil he is!" K.C.'s brows shot up, then he started to laugh. "Never thought the lily-livered snake had a backbone. Now I find he's got fangs."

Kit quickly explained all that had happened in the week since he'd left his company, then handed him the attaché case Phyllis had sent. K.C. silently read his secretary's letter and shuffled through the assortment of papers. "How is Phyl?" he asked, running a hand through his close-cropped hair.

"Her leg is quite bad," Kit told him truthfully. "Her doctor wants to put her in the hospital if it doesn't get better by Tuesday." Kit licked her lips nervously. Her eyes had caught sight of the frantically moving white bag on the plank floor. It had now started hissing. She cleared her throat. "Rafe went to the Mayan dig site looking for you about half an hour ago."

"Well." K.C. frowned, looking out into the gray forest. "It's going to take him at least another half hour to get back here. He'll just about make it before the evening rains hit. I'd better get some supper going."

Kit watched him pick up the sack and head into the kitchen. "Is there . . . is there anything I can help you with?" she asked politely, praying he'd say no.

"Well . . ." He eyed her consideringly. "You could clean off the dining room table. You'll find dishes and silver in the cupboard in the corner. Dinner's going to be my specialty." K.C. grinned, his blue eyes dancing. "Ptomaine stew."

Kit smiled weakly and watched him disappear into the alcove. At the sound of his voice, she quietly peeked into the kitchen and watched K.C. pull a three-foot green iguana from the white bag. The ugly-looking lizard's black-banded tail thrashed angrily. He had inflated his lungs, increasing his size by more than half. "Take it easy," K.C. crooned. "This will only take a second. I guarantee you won't feel a thing."

Kit's eyes widened, her hand clutched her throat, and she ran out on the veranda gasping for air. Ptomaine stews' main ingredient appeared to be iguana!

Half an hour later the stone house was a lit beacon in the dark jungle. K.C. was banging around in the kitchen, cheerfully whistling and singing, seemingly oblivious to the fact that he was dangerously close to losing his company.

Kit prowled anxiously back and forth across the porch, waiting impatiently for Rafe to return. The ever-increasing rumblings of Chac, the Mayan rain god, were growing stronger every minute and the air was heavy with moisture and insects. Kit had drawn blood on numerous spots trying to relieve her itches.

"A light in the window and a fair maiden awaiting my return," drawled a deep, masculine voice. "What more could a man ask for?"

Kit hurled herself against Rafe's rugged body, her arms hugging his neck in relief. "Thank God you're back. I've been so worried. You took so long." Her suppressed fears tumbled from her lips, her eyes feasting on the sight of his familiar face.

Rafe's teeth flashed white in the darkness. His hands roughly caressed her trembling body, pressing it closer into his own. "If I'd known I'd get this reaction, I would have dragged you off into the jungle sooner."

Kit ignored his provocative remark, suddenly embarrassed over her display. She slid out of his embrace and pulled him into the house. "K.C.'s taking things awfully well," she whispered. "He's in the kitchen making ptomaine stew." A shudder passed through her body.

Rafe grinned. "I had that the last time I was here. It's not bad."

Their host came out into the living room, a white

towel tied apronwise around his slim waist. "Thought I heard someone." He smiled and shook Rafe's hand. "Thanks for coming to get me."

"My pleasure," Rafe returned amiably. "How do things look?"

"Not too bad. Phyl is a wonder. Even from a sickbed she rattled a few cages, scared a few birds. I shouldn't have any trouble. I'd like your opinion on a few things."

"Let me get washed and changed," Rafe said, easing the heavily sweat-stained shirt away from his body.

"I'll finish up dinner," K.C. said. "Kit, let me give you some sheets to make up the beds. Or is it bed?" he asked, his eyes twinkling devilishly in his copper face.

"I'm positive the travel agent booked us two separate rooms," she returned tartly, striving to control her heightened color.

K.C. piled clean but rough linen and two pillows into her outstretched arms. "The rooms shouldn't be too bad. Just used them a few days ago when we had to stop work at the dig because of the rain." He handed Rafe a stubby, hand-tied corn broom. "This will chase away any varmints."

Kit followed Rafe down a long hallway that led to two small bedrooms. She took a deep breath and flicked on the light switch, expecting the worst. It wasn't too bad. A double bed filled most of the room. A small chest and mirror were on the far wall and

172

a hemp-seated chair stood under the window. She dumped the sheets on the mattress, then froze, her eyes locked on a lumbering gray-green form that occupied the far corner.

The iguana hissed; the comblike crest of scales down the center of his back stood straight up. A large flap of skin hung from the lizard's throat, and his tail swished silently across the wood floor. Fleetingly, Kit wondered if he was related to tonight's dinner.

Backing out of the room, she turned and stood stiffly in Rafe's doorway. "I think you might need to get a bigger broom," Kit announced, her voice sounding oddly high.

"What's the problem?" he asked, following her across the hall. "That's just a chuckwalla." Rafe laughed, easily catching the slow-moving lizard and depositing it out the window. "They're perfectly harmless." His thumb and forefinger rubbed his mustache reflectively. "And you told me you were a tomboy," he teased.

"I was," Kit retorted, eyeing the corners and crevices in search of other beasties, "but I'm used to New York wildlife—toads, crickets, an occasional garden snake or a field mouse. Not the star of a low-budget dinosaur movie." She ignored his deep chuckle. "I'll make you a deal. You sweep the rooms for creatures and I'll make a bed you can bounce a quarter off of."

The frijoles, corn tortillas, and buñuelos—fried

pancakes—looked very appetizing, and so did the ptomaine stew, rich with chunks of potatoes, onions, peppers, and carrots. Kit eyed the main course with consideration. She was starving but somehow couldn't bring herself to eat iguana. She was glad K.C. and Rafe were engrossed in a business discussion and didn't notice how many buñuelos and tortillas she consumed while deftly pushing the entrée around her plate. Despite the fact that K.C. made coffee strong enough to eat through the glaze of the stone mugs, she found her eyelids drooping and her shoulders sagging under the weight of a sudden lethargy.

"I think the altitude is getting to your girl," K.C. drawled. Rafe leaned over and gently nudged her arm.

Kit gave her head a clearing shake, flushing under her male companions' amused scrutiny. "I think the exercise of doing these dishes will keep me awake for a while." Smiling, she ignored her host's protests, cleared the table, and accomplished the task quickly and efficiently in the tiny kitchen.

It was raining heavily when she returned to the living room. "Do you think we'll have any trouble getting out of here tomorrow?" Kit asked, voicing her growing concerns.

"The rain will stop in an hour," K.C. informed her, then turned to Rafe. "We get an early morning shower, too, which creates a thick fog. We won't be able to get your jeep on that track until about eight.

It'll take a couple of hours for the mud to mold itself into something firmer."

"Even with that delay, we'll get back before noon," Rafe assured him. "I had a good weather report."

Once again, the two men succumbed to business and Kit curled onto a surprisingly comfortable hemp-seated chair, returning to her reading on the Mayan culture. But the multitude of pages on how scientists cracked the ancient language proved to be more of a sedative than a stimulant and she soon fell asleep.

"Come on, Kit. I think you'd better call it a day." Rafe's voice was soft but firm in her ear.

Her eyes fluttered open, and she stretched sleepily, uncurling her long legs from their cramped position. "What time is it?" She felt it had to be near midnight, and wrinkled her nose self-consciously when Rafe informed her it was barely eight thirty. "I haven't gone to bed this early since I was seven," she grumbled, bidding them good night. She headed for her room and a rendezvous with Ah Puch, the reigning god of the evening.

A primitive shriek made Kit sit up, her hands pawing aside the mosquito netting that smothered her face. She reached up and snapped on the small reading light attached to the bed's headboard. The loud call sounded again, and she directed the lamp so that the light bounced off various corners of the room.

She found the culprit—a broken-tailed gecko lizard sedately walking upside down on the rough stucco ceiling—and settled back against the flat pillow, studying the grotesquely dancing shadows on the walls. She was wide awake, completely refreshed after—she glanced at the small travel alarm clock—three hours of sleep. She tried not to give way to twisting and turning, knowing that if she did, any further slumber would be a lost cause.

Part of her mind was trying to concentrate on restful relaxation; another part was aware of the constant grumbling of her stomach. Kit's lips twisted humorously. "A five-foot-ten-inch woman cannot live on tortillas alone," she muttered, thrusting her legs out of the side of the bed and carefully shaking out her slippers before inserting her feet. She slid a navy-blue travel robe over matching sleeveless pajamas and got up. It took a bit of effort to unstick the swollen wooden door, but she accomplished it quietly.

Rafe's bedroom door was closed. The hallway and living room were dark, but there was a shaft of light coming from the kitchen.

"I didn't think two frijoles and three buñuelos could hold you," K.C.'s voice announced cheerfully, his blue gaze swinging from the stove to the tall redhead framed in the alcove.

"I didn't think anyone noticed." Kit grinned self-consciously. Her nose led her feet toward a tantalizing smell wafting from the frying pan. "Umm, chili. It looks good."

"It is good. Pull up a chair."

She hesitated for a moment, then heard her stomach grumble again. "It's not made from leftover iguana, is it?" she asked wistfully.

"Iguana?" His brow puckered in confusion.

"That was the main ingredient in your stew. I saw you take the lizard out of the bag this afternoon and—"

K.C.'s laughter interrupted her. He put the cast-iron pan back on the burner, afraid he'd drop it. "I was tagging the critter for the Wildlife Society, not turning it into dinner." Still chuckling, he reached up and pulled open the cupboard, disclosing a collection of canned goods that rivaled a supermarket display. "This is the basis of ptomaine stew. I just add a few extra vegetables and spices."

"In that case"—she rubbed her hands together and slid into a rope-lashed chair—"dish up a very large plate of chili."

"Be careful, it's hot. Both spicewise and temperaturewise," he cautioned, placing two filled soup bowls on the tiny wooden table. He then filled two glasses with a clear liquid from an earthenware jug marked *Agua,* rimmed the edges of the tumblers with salt, and added a wedge of lime.

The first mouthful of the thick bean-and-beef chili proved hotter in all respects than Kit had anticipated. She made a grab for her glass, quickly draining it. K.C. chuckled, refilled her tumbler, and together they demolished their midnight snack and four glasses of salted lime water in companionable silence.

The ever-whirling ceiling fans had distributed the considerably cooler night air. The spicy chili had warmed Kit's clammy skin, making her feel distinctly relaxed and complacent. K.C. was nice, very nice, she decided. His eyes were forever laughing; his every movement took such little effort. But under all the ease were a simple dignity and a feeling of self-reliance that made him seem very dependable and approachable.

She pushed her dish aside, propped her chin in her hands, and smiled happily at him. "You won't have any trouble holding on to your company, will you?" she asked, her own blue eyes radiating warm concern.

"Nope." K.C. leaned back against the handmade chair and relit his half-smoked cigar. "But this has taught me a lesson. Unlike Rafe, I don't really control my company. I'm only the majority stockholder and have a lot of people to answer to. I've been thinking about getting out completely. I'd have more time to go on digs, go deep-sea fishing, enjoy life. Having a company is like having a wife. It demands that you stick around and participate."

Kit giggled and took another sip of her drink. The *agua* certainly packed a powerful punch, more than any other water she had ever drunk. No wonder everyone warned you about drinking the Mexican resource. Her tongue seemed abnormally large and fuzzy. "Don't you want a wife or a family?"

"Nope." The two front legs of the chair hit the ground, and K.C. poured himself another drink, his movements growing slower, his voice decidedly thicker. "I'm a confirmed bachelor. Like my freedom, like to pack up and go. I spent most of my life prospecting for gold in the hills. You spend so much time with Nature, you become part of her. Nature doesn't want any softies; she's kind but she's cruel. That's the way I am, rough around the edges."

Kit cocked her head, the auburn hair spilling to one side, glowing rich against the navy housecoat. "You're nice, not cruel. I do see kindness. You're honest and direct and, I think, very understanding." She smiled impishly. "What does the K.C. stand for?"

He sucked on the cigar, the burning tobacco crackling under the heat. "Kermit Carson." One blue eye closed, the other glittered an admonishment. "You're the only one I've ever admitted that too. What about Kit? Is that for Katherine or something more exotic?"

She sighed heavily. "Nope, that's it. Short, sweet, and simple. Totally unlike me. I'm long, complicated, and rough around the edges too."

K.C. spit the cigar out of his mouth, the stub landing with perfect accuracy in a pottery spittoon near the stove. His short fingers lifted her chin. Keen eyes surveyed the sweetly rounded contours of her face. "You think you're rough?" He grinned, a gray brow arching speculatively.

She nodded, her full lips taking on a tender droop. "Lousy breeding, blemished pedigree. I was an obnoxious, disruptive, delinquent child. I'm irreverent, impertinent, and a major source of annoyance to almost everyone who gets to know me." She took another gulp of liquid. A pleasant buzzing sound settled in her ears, but it didn't lift the despondency on her face.

"Rafe doesn't think so. After all, you two are engaged—"

Kit shook her head vehemently, then stopped, waiting for her eyeballs to resettle in their sockets. "He doesn't love me. He loves Tracy Shippley and Tracy loves him." The words came out like a child's rhyme, and she found herself giggling. "It doesn't matter. I only cause him a lot of trouble. I cause everybody a lot of trouble. Once we get back, I'm going away."

"Where?" At her unconcerned shrug, K.C. stared broodingly into his glass, his blunt forefinger squeezing the lime against the side of the tumbler. "Listen, if you ever need anything, anything at all, just give me a call."

"Oh, that's so sweet," she moaned, deeply touched by his concern. She hiccuped and clasped her hand over her mouth.

"Hell, I like you kid. You remind me of me." He

grinned, trying to hide his embarrassment. "It's a damn shame you're not twenty years older. I'd turn you into an archaeologist and take you on digs."

"Why don't you take Phyllis?" Kit asked brightly, smiling slyly at his surprised expression. "She's in love with you. She'd follow you around the world, bad leg and all."

"You really think so?" he countered doubtfully, rubbing his fingers across the coarse stubble of beard on his jawline.

"I really do." She nodded confidently. "You know, sometimes you can't see the trees for the forest," she said in a haze of alcoholic wisdom, wagging her finger at him.

K.C. caught her hand and pulled her to her feet. "Hmm, maybe I'll just check that out. I've always had a special feeling for Phyl." He shook his head and smiled ruefully into her flushed face. "Right now, I think we'd both better hit the sack." He gave her a push out the door toward the hall. "Can you find your way back?"

"Of course I can," she intoned with regal dignity that dissolved under another burst of giggles. Impulsively, she kissed his sun-browned cheek, heard him mumble something, then watched him shuffle off to his own room at the far end of the house.

If anything, the hallway seemed longer and darker. Kit bumped her way slowly along the rough stucco walls. One slipper dislodged itself from her foot.

She turned round and round before her toes finally snuggled against the smooth covering.

Dizzily, she groped until her hand curled around the cold metal of a doorknob. "Success!" She giggled, twisting and turning the cylinder only to find that the door refused to budge. She put her shoulder against it, pushing and bouncing, trying to dislodge the swollen wood.

With effort, Kit pondered the situation. *This obviously needs a magic word,* she decided, feeling supremely happy with her besotted decision.

"Abracadabra," she muttered. No, that was for getting rabbits out of hats.

She yawned sleepily. Her palms slapped against the door. "Open Sesame," she gurgled and pushed.

The door pulled open and Kit flew into the room, crashing into something that was solid and warm. It also talked.

"Kit! What the hell!"

Rafe! She looked up, blinked, and smiled. He looked cute and cuddly, wearing nothing but a pair of close-fitting black briefs against the massive expanse of his bronze physique. Her arms wrapped tightly around his neck, throwing them both off balance. Together they tumbled onto the bed.

"Kit!" He shook her shoulders roughly, watching one blue eye slowly open and wink at him. He sighed. "I thought you were sleeping."

She shook her head and kept shaking it until his

hands stopped the movement. "I was midnight-snacking with K.C. He makes non-iguana chili."

"What? Kit, you're not making any sense," he admonished sternly, freeing his neck from her tight grip. "What have you been drinking?" he asked suspiciously.

"*Agua*," she reported dutifully, wriggling the full length of her body onto the soft mattress. "Water with salt and limes. It's good."

Rafe groaned. "That wasn't water, sweetheart. That was K.C.'s homemade raicilla wine. It's more potent than tequila. You are going to have one hell of a headache—" He stopped, shaking his head at her smiling, sleeping face.

He stood looking down at her, his eyes drinking their own form of intoxicant—the tousled mass of fiery curls, the dark fan of lashes against her fair complexion, the rise and fall of her full breasts under the thin pajama covering. She was so much easier to handle this way.

Rafe slid off Kit's robe and pulled the thin sheet over her body. He sighed, then slid his own body next to hers. He moved her head against his chest, his hands curving possessively around her waist. Presently, his dark head fell against her copper one.

CHAPTER NINE

Through the gray swirling mist that clouded her mind, Kit saw him. He had large round ears and a rough toothy smile. The head of a jaguar on the body of a man. His heavy sandaled feet pounded their dance steps in her head. Wielding his battle-ax, chanting his Mayan prayers, he sent legions of lizards and iguanas raining to earth. Chac is falling. Loud shrieks of laughter sounded from the jungle, drowing out the steadily pelting rain.

She groaned, struggling to open her eyes. The heavy lids flickered slowly. The pupils refused to focus even in the dull light. Her eyes closed again, and she snuggled deeper into the warm security of the mattress. It was too bleak, too desolate to get out of bed and much, much too early.

She lifted her hands to her throbbing forehead, letting ten gentle fingers massage away the dull ache. She sighed, feeling relaxed and drowsily content. Ten more fingers, long and firm, spread across her midriff. Warm and strong, they caressed the sensitive skin beneath her pajama top.

Her legs seemed wedged under the weight of two others. But that couldn't be. She only had two legs and two hands. The other set must belong to the extra head she was nursing. Carefully Kit moved, burrowing her cheek against a very solid pillow, a pillow that housed a beating heart!

She struggled to reopen her eyes. Turning, she stared at the pillow. It was bronze and muscular with a heavy mat of dark curly hair. She swallowed and looked up into a pair of amused brown eyes. It was Rafe!

His low, husky voice answered the silent question voiced by her wide, very confused blue eyes. "Your midnight snack with K.C. turned out to be one hundred proof. You ended up crashing into my room and passing out in my bed."

"Oh!" She tried to move her head, but found that his fingers had tangled in her hair, imprisoning her against his chest. "I'm sorry," she mumbled, feeling wholly embarrassed. She wondered if she'd ever outgrow this penchant for getting into outrageous predicaments.

"Don't worry about it," Rafe said cheerfully, his

toes teasing the sensitive soles of her feet. "I find your snoring quite restful."

Kit lay very still, her body curved along the warm length of his. "Do you think the rain will stop soon?"

"It should. It's starting to ease up. It'll take a while for the track to dry out enough to drive on. It's very early yet. Try to get some more sleep."

She couldn't. A small part of her mind sent a silent prayer to Chac, asking the Mayan god for an endless downpour. Then they would have to stay here in the jungle. Away from everyone. Away from reality.

Once they returned to Texas, she'd have to leave. She'd take one more ride on Zodiac, cook one more dinner with Teresa, play one more game of Scrabble with Matt, brush and feed Nosey one last time. Furiously, Kit blinked back the tears that burned under her eyelids.

A cold numbness invaded her bones, and she moved even closer to Rafe, basking in the heat of his body. Tracy would be waiting for him. Kit could never compete with such a lovely, dainty, feminine woman as Tracy. It would be silly, a pipe dream, a fantasy, to even think she could hold on to a man like Rafe.

She swallowed the growing lump constricting her throat, making her head face the truth her heart had known for so long. She was in love with Rafe Morgan! But loving meant giving and she could give him nothing.

Maybe, maybe he wouldn't mind giving her something. The pleasure of a memory. She had known hell; now she wanted to taste a strange new heaven.

This would be their last moment alone. It must be captured or lost forever. Kit decided to capture it. Maybe this would help connect the broken parts of her life, fill in the hollows and bridge the gaps. She stepped over her feelings of inadequacy and insecurity; she swallowed her shyness and inhibitions; she thrust aside her anxiety and fears.

Rafe had wanted her before. Now she wanted him.

Kit turned her face up to his, her eyes wide and luminous, glittering sapphires in the dull light of the bedroom. "Rafe." The throb in her voice echoed the burning ache that had become her body.

His dark eyes gazed questioningly, hungrily, into hers. She pressed her soft, trembling body into his rugged frame, her half-parted lips lightly grazing his firm mouth. He needed no second invitation.

His mouth closed over hers, branding his ownership on her soft lips. The invading thrust of his hard, moist tongue sent wild shivers arcing through her veins. Time dissolved into delicious slow motion. Kit was slowly drowning in an intoxicating sense of well-being under the skilled mastery of his hands.

"I want you, Kit," he demanded hoarsely, his mouth roughly caressing the curve of her cheek, his long fingers quickly dispensing with the four white buttons that held the silken pajama top closed.

"Yes, Rafe," she whispered breathlessly. Her hands roamed lovingly over his chest, luxuriating in the feel of his sinewy muscles, the wiry mat of hair, her fingertips tracing the hardness of his nipples.

She moaned softly, his lips a sweet torture against her arched throat, his mouth seeking the erect tips of her throbbing breasts. His teeth lightly teased the sensitive nipples; his tongue sensuously tormented her burning skin.

"You are so beautiful," he breathed, his voice thick with desire. "I want to see all of you, feel your skin next to mine." In a moment she was freed from her pajama bottoms, he of his briefs.

Her body dissolved into the mattress while his hardened above hers. Kit's fingers pressed against the firm flesh of his back, following his spine to the tough muscles of his buttocks. She lovingly traced the network of scars on his side. "Make me a part of you," she begged shamelessly, arching invitingly beneath him. Her movements came naturally in an urgent desire to feel the ultimate pleasure only his body could give her.

Her words inflamed him even more. "You are mine," he stated fiercely. His mouth rained kisses over her flat stomach, her flushed breasts, and her waiting lips. His leg parted her silken thighs. He took her hand, guiding her, showing her where to touch him. She felt him quiver with pleasure.

"Rafe!" she breathed, her hips surging forward against the long finger that had invaded the moist center of her passion. She shuddered, feeling sensations she had never before known existed.

Suddenly Rafe loomed over her; his face filled her eyes. She gasped when he entered her. His mouth captured hers, consuming her brief moment of discomfort. He remained perfectly still, savoring the moment of her sweet surrender.

Kit had lost herself. She couldn't tell where her body ended and Rafe's began. There was no room, no walls, no jungle, no time, no space—everything around her was obliterated in the wonder of sensual delight.

She felt him move inside her—slow strokes, delicate at first, then growing more and more powerful. His lovemaking was an unfolding, every gesture showing he was fully absorbed in their mutual pleasure. Her body vibrated around his. Kit's arm crept tightly around his neck, clinging to his solid form; she needed him so much it was frightening.

He lifted her hips, moving her tighter against his thrusting desire. Her body and soul lifted from within. She dissolved into a small series of rhythmic movements that blotted out her very self. The pleasure mounted so intensely, she thought she would explode. Then suddenly she did. Her body shook, her fingers convulsively dug into his shoulders. His body erupted, pulsating and quaking under his release. His weight came down on top of her.

Rafe's breathing was deep and ragged. His lips gently kissed her swollen, flushed nipples, moving to her trembling mouth before closing her fluttering eyelids. *"Solamente una vez se entrega el alma con la*

189

dulce y total renunciación." His voice was low and unsteady in her ear.

Shyly, Kit moved her head onto his chest, content in the warm strength of his arms. "What does that mean?" she asked softly.

"It's the words to a Mexican song," he murmured, pulling her tightly against him as his fingers brushed back her tangled hair. "Only once does the soul surrender completely and so sweetly."

A sweet surrender? Kit's inner critical voice echoed Rafe's words in her subconscious. She had not surrendered. She had taken. She had used Rafe's body. She had forced his tender embraces and passionate words.

Sweet! The voice cackled hysterically, shattering the tranquil silence of her mind. She had never been sweet or kind or generous. She was a liar and a user.

A cold tension grew inside her. How could she have done this to him? She had used him to satisfy her own needs and feelings. He didn't deserve that. She had already taken so much from him.

What had she given him? She had no experience to offer, no way to satisfy him. She came to him like a sacrificial Mayan maiden—an uneducated body, a piece of stone.

He was so quiet, Kit thought, but what could he say? She was obviously a poor substitute for Tracy, and it was stupid to think this was anything other than a physical release for him. She had forced sex to do the work of love. Once again she had created an illusion. She had succumbed to another fantasy, thinking she might be able to hold on to him. To stay in his world.

She was lying to herself this time, being dishonest. She had no future with Rafe. If anything, she felt more lonely and rejected than ever. Kit began to tremble, fighting the bitter self-condemnation that formed in her throat.

She became a moving mass of arms and legs. Jumping from the bed, she grabbed her navy robe and pajamas from the tangled white sheets, clutching them protectively against her body. "I'm sorry. I am so sorry," she stammered.

"Kit!" Startled, Rafe sat up.

She put her hand to her mouth and shook her head, then bolted for the door. Seconds later, she was in her own bedroom. She pushed a handmade chair under the doorknob. Out in the hallway a door opened. Kit heard footsteps. She held her breath, her eyes watching the door, her ears tuned to the slightest sound, her body a twitching mass of nerves.

Then she heard another voice. It was K.C. calling Rafe. Relief flooded through every pore and Kit collapsed onto her bed.

She dressed slowly, her shaking fingers struggling with the buttons of her madras blouse and catching the zipper of her jeans. She could smell Rafe on her body. Despite the heat, she shivered, the inherent masculine scent recalling the carnal memories of minutes ago.

The more she thought about what she'd done, the more distraught she became. Her actions had been deliberate and willful. She had taken advantage of Rafe to assuage her own feelings. She rubbed her aching forehead. She seemed to have acquired a splitting headache; even blinking had become painful.

A few hours ago, she had prayed to stay here. Now she couldn't wait to leave—to get back to the ranch, pack her things, and leave all the memories behind. Only when she heard K.C. clattering pans in the kitchen did Kit leave the safety of her room.

"Good morning." K.C. smiled cheerfully, looking up from the four eggs he was frying on the stove. "Rafe's packing the jeep. I see you're all set. How about some breakfast?" He stopped, raised his gray brow, his eyes studying her grim expression. "Maybe you'd rather have a little hair of the dog?"

Kit shook her head, the side of her cheek flickering under the pain of that simple movement. "No, coffee will be fine." She was relieved that he thought her subdued behavior came from a hangover. She gave him a weak smile, gratefully accepting the steamy mug of coffee. He looked different this morning. Gone was the Mexican Indian attire. In its place were a pair of worn Levi's jeans, a blue denim workshirt, and a suede vest polished by age to a high gloss.

K.C. settled in the chair across from her, sprinkling chili pepper on top of the hard-cooked egg yolks. "Have you thought any more about where you're going?" he asked.

"California," she heard herself say. Why not? It was as good a place as any to start over.

"My offer of last night still stands," he told her, leveling a compelling blue gaze in her pensive face. "I know a few people out there who can help you find a job and a place to live. Stop and see me before you take off. That's an order," he added.

Kit looked at him and licked her lips, her voice thick with unaccustomed emotion. "Thanks. I don't really deserve your kindness. I—" She stopped at the sound of the front door opening and boots echoing across the floor.

"The jeep's all set and the track looks pretty solid." Rafe's warm, large hand settled on her shoulder. "Is your suitcase ready, Kit?"

She held herself perfectly taut, her eyes focusing on a chameleon that was walking across the far wall. She stubbornly refused to look at him, her voice more remote than ever. "I left it by the front door."

"Fine." His hand lifted, the boots walked away. Kit took a deep breath. K.C. shook his head, picked up her cup and his dish, and walked to the sink.

Only Rafe's skillful driving prevented them from getting stranded in the muddy jungle road. Kit, who was wedged in the backseat, felt every jounce and bounce reverberate the entire length of her frame. By the time they arrived at the airport in Villahermosa, her every joint and muscle ached severely. Her arms and legs were cold, but the rest of her body felt as if it were on fire. She collapsed into the first passenger seat in the plane, leaving K.C. to join Rafe in the tiny cockpit.

The air pressure threatened not only to rupture Kit's eardrums but to explode her brain as well. The migraine she was suffering had turned every blink of an eyelid into pure agony. Her legs were racked with muscle spasms and her skin seemed unbearably sensitive to even the slightest weight.

Her clothes, the seat belt, the velour cushion of the chair were torture against her body. The cabin, which had been comfortable on the flight over, had now become unbelievably cold. It was an exercise in concentration just to stop shivering.

Rafe opened the cream folding door that separated the cockpit from the cabin, bending his tall frame against the low slope of the cabin. He stopped in front of Kit's stiffly sitting figure. "How are you doing?" he asked politely.

"Fine."

"We'll be landing at the ranch in half an hour. I'll drop you there and then fly K.C. into town." He cleared his throat, his hand nervously wiping his mustache and upper lip. "Can I get you anything?"

"No."

Rafe's forehead puckered. He continued to stare at the rigid set of her body and the fixed, unblinking eyes. He dropped to his haunches, cleared his throat again, and squeezed her arm. "Look, Kit—"

Her breath caught in her throat, her flesh shrank from his fingers. Whatever affliction she was suffer-

194

ing from seemed a fitting punishment. This morning she had begged Rafe to touch her. Now the feel of his hand was pure torment. "Don't!" Kit whispered.

Rafe's voice snapped in the quiet cabin. "What the hell is the matter with you?" he growled savagely, staring at her impassive features. He lowered his head. "This morning you begged me to love you. Now you won't look at me, you won't talk to me—"

"Just forget about this morning. I have. It was nothing," she returned firmly, shivering against the stream of perspiration that dribbled down her spine. The muscles around her mouth twitched painfully under her spoken lie.

He swore harshly and lunged to his feet. "I don't know why the hell I even bother. You're not worth the trouble."

Miserably, she watched him stalk back to the cockpit. She was almost glad he was angry. It was better this way. It made leaving so much easier. Rafe had every right to hate her. She hated herself.

It was Matt who drove her back to the ranch, teasing her about her poor flying ability. Kit suffered the anguish of another bone-shattering jeep ride across rolling terrain. She had never felt so weak and aching in all her life, or more depressed. Her throat was sore and tender against every swallow. Her clothes had become glued to her burning, wet skin.

When Matt pulled up to the cottage's front porch, Kit literally fell out of the jeep, her knees buckling under her weight. "Don't worry," she told him, assuaging his swiftly mounting concern. "It's just airsickness. A couple of aspirin and a long nap on something stationary will do me a world of good."

She pushed Nosey aside, unable to stand the pressure of his paws against her sensitive legs, and groped her way along the hall toward the bedroom. *It's just the flu,* Kit told herself. *A little rest and you'll be fit enough to leave.* She collapsed across the bed.

K.C.'s nose twitched appreciatively as he followed Rafe into the living room of the sprawling Morgan hacienda. "Dinner smells terrific. I'm glad you talked me into coming back here tonight."

"You deserved a celebration. I never saw a man shrivel the way your nephew did when you walked into your office today." Rafe handed him a drink, lifting his own glass in a silent toast.

The older man chuckled reminiscently, savoring the smooth bourbon that rolled over his tongue. "Well, the more I think about it, the less mad I get. Actually, with a little training, Nephew George may make a good successor. He just has to learn not to jump the gun."

"Are you really going to retire?" Rafe asked, settling into a gold chair.

"I was telling Kit that I'd really like to. I've got a few good years left in me and I'd like to enjoy them, not let the confines of an office smother me." K.C. cocked his head at the quiet that permeated the house. "Where is Kit, anyway? I know she'll be interested to hear what happened, and I want to tell her that I managed to talk Phyl into going to the hospital. Maybe Kit will come with me later when visiting hours start."

"She's probably helping Teresa in the kitchen," Rafe muttered, his brooding gaze directed into his Scotch. There was a movement by the door and he looked up expectantly, but only to find Matt. "How'd your day go?"

"Not too bad." Matt grinned, pouring himself a ginger ale. "You can leave me in charge with confidence."

"You better watch that boy, Rafe." K.C. chuckled. "That's exactly what my nephew said to me."

Teresa announced dinner and the three men followed the housekeeper into the dining room, settling themselves at the food-laden table. Rafe stared morosely at the one vacant chair. "Is Kit still in the kitchen?"

Teresa shook her head, her brows rising in surprise. "Why, no. I haven't seen her all day. I thought she was with you."

"Matt," Rafe barked, his voice ragged as if pulled from deep within his chest, "you didn't take her into town, did you?"

Matt looked up from buttering a dinner roll and shook his head. "She barely made it into the cottage, Uncle Rafe. I never saw anyone so airsick. She said she was going to rest, and I've been busy in the far pasture. I thought she was helping Teresa the way she always does."

Rafe led a procession of three across the back patio to the darkened guest cottage. He knocked on the back door, pushing his way in when he received no reply. "Kit!" The house echoed with silence. A burning knot twisted in his stomach; it was beginning to look as if she had left.

Nosey's loud whining directed their attention to the bedroom. Rafe snapped on the ceiling light. Four pairs of eyes stared at the bed. Teresa hastily crossed herself, mumbling in Spanish. K.C. looked at Rafe, who was holding Matt at bay.

Kit was sprawled across the mattress, her clothes plastered to her body with perspiration. She was tossing fitfully, sobbing under each painful movement. The soulful-eyed schnauzer lay at her side.

Kit whimpered like a beaten animal under the weight of the cool, gentle hand Rafe lay against her burning, damp forehead. "Matt," he directed urgently, "call Dr. Demarest and tell him to get here fast."

John Demarest eyed the four pacing figures indulgently. "You can all relax," he smiled, pulling off his stethoscope and opening his black medical bag. "Kit doesn't have typhoid or malaria or yellow fever. Although she could have. I found four ticks boring their way through the back of her neck and she's loaded with insect bites. Where the hell did you drag that poor girl, Rafe?"

198

"Well . . . we . . . I . . ." Rafe sighed heavily, running a weary hand under his own damp shirt collar. "What the hell has she got?"

"Breakbone fever," John told him. "It's the thirty-fifth case in this area in the last two months. It looks much worse than it really is." He smiled reassuringly at the doubtful-looking housekeeper and patted Teresa's arm comfortingly. "She's got a very high fever and will need to be sponged down. Try and get lots of liquids into her, Teresa." John handed Rafe a bottle of medication. "I gave her a shot for the pain and to lower the fever, but Kit's got a long seventy-two hours ahead of her. She's delirious and very weak and in a lot of pain."

For the next three days Kit was barely conscious of all the action that surrounded her. Her heat-lacerated brain propelled her though a tangled labyrinth of blurred faces, hollow voices, and a myriad of aesthetic sensations. She sobbed in relief at the gentle ministering hands that sponged her aching, feverish skin and changed her perspiration-soaked night-gowns and sheets for fresh, dry linen.

She seemed to slip into numerous dreams; visions of the past danced crazily in her mind. Angry voices grew louder and louder, screaming and cursing at her. Even Rafe's normally laughing, teasing face was etched in harsh, forbidding lines. "You're trouble, too much trouble," he told her.

Kit clamped her hands to her ringing ears and

bolted upright, her lungs gasping for air, her eyes wide and frightened.

"Take it easy." Two strong hands settled on her shoulders, gently guiding her back against the pillows.

She blinked, her eyes trying to focus on the shadowy figure in the dimly lit room. She recognized Rafe's voice. Her own voice was a dry whisper. "Where am I? What happened?"

Rafe sat down on the edge of the bed. "You're doing just fine. You had a very bad fever but the worst is over." He reached up and switched on the low reading lamp. "I brought you into the main house. You're in my room."

Kit wet her cracked lips with her tongue. "I'm sorry. I didn't mean to get sick. I—" His fingers against her mouth silenced her.

"Stop apologizing," he returned brusquely. "Here, take this." Rafe handed her two pills and held a glass of fruit juice to her lips.

Kit's eyes never left his face. He looked so grim and angry. Obediently she swallowed the pills and cool juice but that brief bit of exercise sapped her strength, and she collapsed against the mattress. "I'm sorry," she murmured despondently. "I'm always so much trouble. I'll be better soon, I promise."

Rafe cursed softly, tucking the bedclothes around her as if she were a child. "Just rest. Don't worry about a thing. I'm right here if you need anything."

Kit's eyes closed under the heavy burden of medication, but Rafe's scowling image continued to plague her.

A second fever heralded a pink rash that threatened to rival her hair in brilliance. By the following Monday the itchy rash had scaled off, her temperature was back to normal, and her appetite had returned. Despite Teresa's audible misgivings, Dr. Demarest approved her request to rejoin the living.

Kit felt smug about surprising everyone at lunch. She had managed a refreshing shower and shampoo and had dressed herself in a pair of green cotton slacks and a print top. It was one of the outfits Rafe had bought her. She had found the entire wardrobe of clothes still hanging in his closet.

The hairbrush grew unbearably heavy in her hand. She placed it on Rafe's dresser and stared at herself in the wide mirror. The fever had taken the sheen out of her copper hair and the sparkle from her blue eyes. Her face looked haggard and splotchy from the rash. The clothes hung on her body from the weight she had lost. The doctor had said she would be exhausted and depressed for two weeks, but she suspected that the melancholy she was feeling had little to do with her illness.

Now that she was recovering, Kit had to face the realization that she would have to leave the ranch very soon. Rafe had been very attentive during the past week, but she could no longer impose on him. He would probably be relieved when she left, she had caused him so much trouble. His words still echoed in her mind and Kit dismally wondered how she was going to find the courage to face him.

It took her a bit longer to negotiate the stairs than she had anticipated. Her legs seemed waffly at times, and beads of perspiration soon clung to her forehead under the stress of her efforts. She leaned against the wooden banister, pausing to catch her breath, thinking how tired Teresa must have been from the endless trips she had made upstairs each day to care for her.

An increasing volume of voices coming from the living room caught her attention. Kit's bare feet silently crossed the earth-colored terrazzo-tiled foyer. She stood to one side of the partially open carved doors, her blue eyes widening at the sight of Tracy Shippley's petite figure pacing back and forth across the Oriental carpet.

"Now I realize she has been very sick. But how long are you going to let that woman take advantage of you?" Tracy said shrilly. "She's got this whole household in an uproar. You haven't been at work all week. None of your friends have been able to get in touch with you. Really, she is just taking advantage of your good nature." She stopped pacing and eyed the stucco wall consideringly, her small hands unnecessarily reaching out to straighten an oil painting.

She turned and smiled, the sunlight glinting on her shimmering blond hair and perfect features, her dainty white gauze dress with its delicate crocheted straps and trim making her look unbelievably fragile

202

and feminine. "Rafe," Tracy cooed, her mascara-darkened lashes fluttering appealingly, "this whole engagement business is just ridiculous. She is nothing. You cannot be serious about her." She sighed, her hand straying to the square neckline of her dress. "Now, I know how uncomfortable you must be having her around, but I can take care of that for you. You are just too tolerant and easygoing to ask her to leave."

Rafe walked over, his hands settling heavily on Tracy's graceful shoulders, his dark gaze studying her ethereal features. He grinned suddenly, the dimples deepening in his cheeks, the brown eyes taking on a glow. "You know, you are quite right. This nonsense can't go on forever," he agreed cheerfully. "I have been very patient, very tolerant, and very lenient."

Kit's heart stopped; she needed to hear no more. Quickly and quietly, her feet led her through the house to the guest cottage. Everything was exactly the way she had left it. She stripped off the clothes Rafe had purchased, replacing them with her own tan slacks and a black T-shirt, then slid her feet into a pair of comfortable sandals, found her purse, and located the carry-all that was still packed from her Mexico trip.

She was sweating profusely, but her inherent strength pushed aside her body's physical weakness. She didn't need Tracy Shippley to toss her out; she was perfectly capable of leaving by herself. And she was going to do it right now!

Kit made her way to the garage but found that none of the vehicles had keys in their ignitions. It would take a taxi over an hour just to get out here. Who else could she call? She had virtually lost touch with her friends, Nancy and Jeanne. She thought of calling Gretchen Stanford but then decided the situation would be awkward since her husband was Rafe's friend.

Kit heard the sounds of clanking metal and voices chattering rapidly in Spanish. Sliding along the back of the house, she spotted a delivery truck. The driver was just turning the engine over; the back of the flatbed truck beckoned to her. She tossed in her purse and tote bag, gritted her teeth, and pulled herself onto the dirty floorboards. The gears ground and the truck lumbered across the gravel drive, picking up speed once the tires hit macadam.

Her heart was pounding in her ears, her breathing rapid under such exertions. Kit leaned her weary body against a lumpy sack of potatoes. The sun was hot and strong, beating against her uncovered head and hammering her eyes into slits. She managed to arrange her shoulder bag as an awning to shield her face and head from the heat, then gave herself up to blissful slumber as the truck moved out onto the highway.

CHAPTER TEN

Kit's fingers hastily combed through her rumpled hair and brushed off her dusty clothes. She stepped out of the elevator and took a deep breath, trying to garner enough poise to confront the bored-looking receptionist. "I'd like to see Mr. Whittier, please," she said.

"Do you have an appointment?" the elfin-faced brunette rasped in a nasal tone, her eyes briefly lifting from her magazine.

"No. No, I don't. But if you tell him it's Kit Forrester, I'm sure he'll see me."

The young woman looked up, her brown eyes narrowing in disapproval at the tall, disheveled redhead. "I'm sorry. If you don't have an appointment

. . ." Her voice trailed off, her gaze refocusing on the glossy printed page.

"I'm a very close friend of K.C.'s," Kit said firmly, her tone grim with determination. "He'll be very upset if you don't announce me." Her hands were gripping the wooden overhang of the free-form oak desk, her body still shaky from the two-hour truck ride and the four-block walk she had undertaken to get to K.C.'s office building.

The receptionist sucked in her cheeks, reached over, and picked up the telephone. She spoke quietly for a moment, frowned, then looked up with an exclamation of surprise when the inner office door was flung open.

"Kit!" K.C. gasped, striding into the beige and brown reception area. "What the devil are you doing here?"

"I need a favor," she said, smiling in relief at the comforting sight of his face. He looked every inch the successful executive in his light blue business suit, white shirt, and striped tie. "The banks are all closed and—"

"Come in here." He waved her silent, ushering her into the privacy of his own luxurious office. "Sit down, you look ready to collapse," he ordered, pushing her toward a rust velour sofa. He walked over to a small corner bar and poured her a glass of ice water. "What are you doing here? You should still be in bed."

Kit gulped the water greedily, sighed, and leaned

against the soft cushions. "I'm all right, really. I just need some money to get away. I can write you a check. I didn't expect the banks to be closed and—" She stopped, realizing she was babbling and making little sense. She rubbed the damp glass against her forehead, willing herself to control her emotions.

"Take it easy." K.C. patted her hand reassuringly. "What happened? What makes it so important that you leave?"

Feeling a wave of desolation and sickness crash over her, Kit pulled herself together, her voice jerky. "I came downstairs hoping to surprise everyone, only I got the surprise. Rafe and Tracy were in the living room and I heard them talking. I was going to leave, I told you that." She clutched at his arm, her voice gulping back sobs. "But he was going to let her send me away, and I couldn't take that. I hid in the back of a truck and came into town."

"What!" K.C. jumped off the arm of the sofa, rocking back and forth on the heels of his leather boots. "Why, that lousy bastard! I thought for sure he—"

"Don't say that," Kit breathed, wiping away the tears with the back of her hand. "That's what was supposed to happen. Rafe was always trying to get Tracy back. It wasn't his fault that I fell in love with him." She sniffed and exhaled. "Look, if you could just loan me the money, I can get a bus out of town. I hate to ask you, I've been so much trouble to everyone and—"

"Just shut up," he said not unkindly, returning to his seat on the arm of the sofa. "You haven't been a bit of trouble, and you're in no condition to go anywhere. You need at least a couple weeks of rest, some sunshine, and good food." K.C. looked at his watch, his mouth twisting speculatively. "I'm on my way to Corpus Christi to put the finishing touches on a business deal. I'm taking you with me," he announced, smiling at her startled expression. "I've got a fishing shack on Aransas Bay. It's the perfect spot for you to rest."

"K.C., I can't let you—"

"Oh, yes, you can," he interrupted brusquely, his gnarled fingers wiping the wetness from her cheeks. "Phyl is still in the hospital so I know she's well taken care of. Now I'm going to see to it that you're taken care of." He grinned suddenly, his blue eyes dancing mischievously. "I suppose people will talk if I adopt you."

Kit laughed, then started to cry, a procession of fat tears burning down her gaunt cheeks. "I don't know why you're so nice to me. You came to see me every night while I was sick. I don't deserve this. I—"

"Come on now, just stop this," he ordered gruffly. "We can pick up a few things for you on the way. The woman who takes care of the house can stay with you. I'll—"

Kit shook her head. "I've put enough people out already. I can manage myself. Honest, I'm fine. I think once I get some rest and start eating again, I'll be back to normal in no time." K.C. eyed her doubtfully, then reluctantly capitulated under her continued pleading.

The fishing shack turned out to be a three-bedroom house with a charming galley kitchen, a Greatroom with a massive stone fireplace, and sliding glass doors that overlooked the Intercoastal Waterway. The shimmering waters of the Gulf of Mexico lay in the distance, and although the area was home to the Aransas National Wildlife Refuge, it also had natural gas collection batteries, oil wells, and pumping facilities.

At dusk the coral and pink sky was in tumult with egrets, herons, terns, and gulls. Each morning the raucous calls of the black skimmers acted as Nature's alarm clock, heralding the start of a new day.

Armed with a collection of K.C.'s nature books and his powerful binoculars, Kit spent her days crunching along the shell-strewn beach. She found a reddish egret nesting on top of a yucca and painstakingly logged rough sketches of the colorful butterflies that inhabited the area.

Such activities kept her occupied, at least during the day. Her nights were a different story. Then dreams took control. Whirling memories haunted her sleep. Alone in the dark, it was Rafe's bed she was sleeping in; his hands were holding her body; his mouth was warm against her lips.

She woke each day with an aching loneliness twisting like a knife into her soul. She sought refuge in the knowledge that depression was one of the aftereffects of her fever. In time, maybe she would find peace.

K.C. called her at least twice a day. She dutifully gave him an hour-by-hour report of her activities. It was silly, but for the first time she felt she had acquired a parent who was concerned about her welfare. She was enjoying the attention.

Phyllis was due to be released from the hospital in another week, and under K.C.'s ministerings both his "girls" were going to rest together. Kit found herself looking forward to Phyl's arrival.

It was an incredibly beautiful day. Great blue herons dotted the vivid azure sky, the long strokes of their labored wings sending them out toward the gulf. Kit followed the short gravel road to the marina's small general store that provided her with all of her supplies.

During her week on Aransas Bay, the sun had given her a golden tan and the fishermen had provided her with nutritious meals that had restored her lost weight. Physically she was doing quite well; mentally and emotionally she was barely coping.

Chet Arnold, the gravel-voiced, full-bearded ex-sailor who ran the grocery store, greeted her warmly. He had adopted her too, and now Kit followed him around the crowded shop, letting him fill her shopping bag with the best of his produce, fresh fruit, and a jug of milk. Chet also insisted on giving her a pound of freshly caught giant shrimp that he had cleaned and shelled. She smiled her appreciation and added a cold can of soda to her purchases before venturing outside the air-conditioned store to greet the increasing heat of the morning.

Excited yips and barking captured her attention. Kit looked down from the weathered store porch and saw a schnauzer hanging out the half-opened window of a parked car. For an instant she thought it was Nosey, but on closer inspection she realized this dog was smaller and darker and had cropped ears. Still, the boxy face and liquid brown eyes brought a prickling of tears to her eyelids. She found herself running the two blocks to the beachside cottage.

She stepped into the cool comfort of the house, slamming the door behind her. Her khaki shorts and green T-shirt were drenched, partly from perspiration but mostly from the soda, which had erupted all over her.

She put away all the perishables, went into the bedroom, stripped off her clothes, and stood under the cooling comfort of the shower massage. The warm needles of pulsating water eased the tension from her shoulders and neck. Wrapped in a giant brown bath towel, Kit fell exhausted onto the king-size bed. It had been stupid to exert herself over the sight of one little dog. She buried her face in the softness of the giant pillow, closing her mind to the memories.

Something landed on the bed and bounced across

the mattress. He was silver and furry and whining with happiness. Two white paws held down her shoulders while a warm pink tongue and cold nose assaulted her face in a boisterous greeting.

Kit blinked and stared into Nosey's alert face. No one had told her insanity was also a by-product of the fever. Up until now her dreams had never been three-dimensional. She closed her eyes again, her hands coming to calm the the frisky animal. It was just her imagination, she told herself calmly. Only a dream.

The mattress was depressed again, this time with a heavier weight. Reluctantly she flicked her eyes open, wondering what manifestation would next assail her.

A man was seated on the edge of the bed. He had dark wavy hair, warm brown eyes, and a thick mustache highlighting his rugged features. He was wearing a navy knit shirt and jeans and holding a bag of dog food and a dish. She closed her eyes again. Her mind had snapped!

"The first thing you are going to do is feed this poor dog. He hasn't eaten a thing since you left. He's starving."

Kit started violently and sat up. She reached out, her hand coming in contact with warm flesh. It *was* Rafe. He was here and very real.

His velvety brown eyes darkened sensuously. "The dog's not the only one who's starving. I'm hungry too, but not for food. You're going to have to appease

212

my appetite very shortly, but it's going to take a lifetime to satisfy it."

Rafe bent over and removed his boots, dropping them with a resounding thud that echoed across the plank floor. He pulled off his shirt, tossing it in the direction of a nearby chair, then stood up, his fingers going to the silver buckle of his belt. "Now I realize keeping a woman barefoot and pregnant these days is against Gloria Steinem, the ERA, and the entire feminist movement. But so help me, Kit, if that's the only way I can keep you firmly shackled to my side, I'm going to have a hell of a lot of fun doing it."

She stared at him for a moment, then with a little sob hurled herself into his arms, dragging him back onto the bed. His arms were familiar bands of steel that encircled her trembling body. She burrowed her face in the warm curve of his shoulder, inhaling the clean, male scent of his skin, loving the feel of his firm, smooth flesh beneath her fingers.

Tears blurred her eyes and she wept against his shoulder. Rafe let her cry for a few minutes, then pulled her away, his fingertips brushing away the dampness from her pale, strained face. She stared at him, letting her eyes drink in every plane and angle of his face. He looked haggard and tired.

Rafe's hands curved around her bare shoulders, and he smiled softly. "Kit, will you kindly tell me what made you run away? My God, this has been the worst week of my life."

She swallowed, her face a controlled mask as she

remembered the scene she had overheard. She flinched from the comfort of his body, her fingers wrapping the bath towel around her protectively. "The worst week of your life," she countered belligerently. "I heard you and Tracy discussing how to get rid of me. I was not trying to take advantage of you and I was not going to let that woman toss me out. I left on my own." Her voice faltered, her eyes shifting to Nosey, who was busily gobbling up the dry dog food that had spilled across the floor. "I'm not going back to playing your fiancée, Rafe Morgan," Kit announced, raising her glittering blue eyes to his, her face drawn and unhappy.

He smiled lazily, his finger tracing the mutinous line of her soft mouth. "That's just fine, sweetheart. If you had eavesdropped a few minutes longer, you would have heard me tell a very shocked Miss Shippley exactly who I thought was taking advantage of me." His voice had roughened; his eyes were narrowing grimly. "I told her in very ungentlemanly language what I thought of that letter she wrote and the way she had treated you."

Kit shook her head, her eyes mirroring her confusion. "I don't understand any of this. You were the one who—"

Rafe's mouth effectively swallowed her words and assuaged her doubts. She gave a sigh of resignation, winding her arms around his strong neck, her fingers lovingly tangling in his springy dark hair. The bath towel slipped unheeded to her waist. Her soft breasts were crushed against his sinewy, hair-roughened chest.

He pushed her down into the soft depths of the mattress, his masterful hands caressing the satiny length of her back, molding her pliant form tightly against his. His mouth left her eager lips to blaze a fiery trail to her rosy-peaked breasts. "Kit," he groaned huskily, "I love you. I don't know what else to do or how else to say it."

She lay quietly in his arms for a long moment, unable to believe what he had just said. Her hands cupped his face, her eyes shining their answer. "I love you. I love you so much. I've been slowly dying without you. I don't want to be away from you ever again."

His arms tightened convulsively, pulling her even closer. "That's just fine." He kissed her soundly. "We are going to pack up and go home. Since we've already been engaged, we're going to get married right away."

"Do I get Nosey as a wedding present?" Kit asked, her eyes twinkling mischievously, her tongue darting out to lightly trace the sensuous curve of his mouth.

"I get the distinct impression that I'm being manipulated," he growled playfully, his white teeth gently nipping the sensitive skin of her swelling breasts. "Yes, you may have the pup."

She eluded his seeking mouth, her hands pushing against his broad chest, rolling him onto his back.

"I'm suddenly getting the feeling that I'm the one who's been manipulated," Kit charged ruefully, pointedly ignoring the raw passion in his eyes. "I still have a million questions that need answers."

"Only a million?" Rafe grinned, his hands repositioning her naked body on line with his. "Go ahead, ask away."

With extreme difficulty Kit ignored the hardening length beneath her. "When did you decide you were not in love with Tracy?" she demanded, folding her arms across his chest.

"I was never in love with Tracy."

Her jaw dropped, and she shook her head. "What do you mean you were never in love with her?" she echoed. "Her sister told me you two were practically engaged. You wanted her to go on the cruise with you. It was your idea to bring her to heel using me."

His fingers gently tugged a long curling strand of russet hair. "I don't care what the little blond bookends told you. I was never engaged to Tracy. I saw her on exactly five occasions—three at her parents' house while I was conducting business with Jack and twice on my own," Rafe admitted. "That's all it took. You see, she gives me a headache, too."

"But what about the cruise?"

"Tracy invited herself. When I said no, she flounced off to New York with her mother, more embarrassed than anything else," he said judiciously. "Actually, you were the one who gave me the idea about the phony engagement."

"I was?" She blinked rapidly.

Rafe nodded. "I told you I had checked you out long before I saw you at Shippley's party. After talking with you, I was thoroughly convinced that you really had made up that wild story to save face with your friends and that using my name was just an accident. A very lucky accident." He kissed the tip of her nose, letting his hands roam over her back and settle on her curving buttocks.

"When I got back to the ranch that night, I couldn't get you out of my mind. I hated that tiny, cramped attic you were living in, and started to worry about you walking around in that neighborhood. I made up my mind to do something about it. I put the note in the gossip column myself," he admitted, dismissing her shocked gasp with a bold, unrepentant grin. "I had a gut feeling that behind that feisty exterior beat a compassionate heart. And when you concluded that your lie had sparked my estrangement, I jumped on it, figuring I would bide my time and wait for you to start feeling something for me."

"But, Rafe," Kit chided gently, her fingers toying with the dark mat of hair on his chest, "you couldn't possibly have fallen in love with me that very first night."

"I didn't know exactly what I felt," he admitted huskily, his lips gently caressing her chin. "I was attracted to you. I couldn't understand why I was so worried about you. The longer I was around you, the faster I found myself falling in love with you. You were direct, warm, witty, and, sometimes, honest. But whenever I got too close, you bolted. I found myself playing a game of advance and retreat."

She laid her cheek against his chest, marveling at the way their two hearts beat as one. "I thought you were in love with Tracy and just using me to relieve a tense libido, especially since you knew about my mother," Kit confessed quietly. "No one has ever wanted me, no one has ever loved me. I didn't recognize it when I saw it or when I felt it." She raised her troubled eyes to his face. "You are saddling yourself with a very insecure person. I have always been more trouble than I've been worth and—"

She gave a startled cry as Rafe flipped her over, pinning her roughly underneath the considerable weight of his body. "I don't ever want to hear that again," he growled savagely. "I realize I said those words to you, but I was angry and confused myself and didn't realize how sick you were." He relaxed his grip on her waist, letting the passionate touch of his mouth erase all the bitter words they had shared. "I would like to know what was going on in your brain that morning in the jungle when you bolted out of my bed."

Kit felt her cheeks suffuse with color. She wound her arms tightly around his neck. "I was feeling guilty about using you," she explained, then sighed at his puzzled frown. "I had planned on leaving when we flew back. I couldn't stay any longer and watch you with Tracy. I . . . I . . ." She licked suddenly dry lips and lowered her eyes from his unwavering stare. "I loved you and I wanted you to love me, even if it was only a physical release for you. I'm afraid I didn't do very well. I didn't have any experience. I didn't satisfy you. I just lay there like a stone . . ." Her voice trailed off miserably. She felt his shoulders shake with laughter and looked up suspiciously.

A finger beneath her chin tipped her head back so that his mouth could fasten on her lips. "You did not lie there like a stone," Rafe teased, his nose rubbing against hers. "For the first time in my life I had made love to a woman and not just had sex. I found that immensely satisfying," he added, his voice low and vibrating with the depth of his sincerity.

Kit purred contentedly, snuggling against him, her toes wiggling under the pant leg of his jeans to tease his warm flesh. "I'm so very glad you're here."

"Let me tell you something, sweetheart. Finding you was the most formidable task I've ever undertaken," Rafe growled, giving her a threatening little shake. "Teresa, Matt, and I searched the ranch for hours, thinking you might have had a relapse and collapsed under the hot sun."

"I didn't think about that," she said contritely. "And after all Teresa has done for me. Do you think she'll ever forgive me?"

"Forgive you?" He laughed out loud. "She's mad as hell at me. She knew Tracy was in the house and, like you, she put two and two together and came up with five. Matt's the same. He's barely civil. Even the damn dog kept growling at me. And K.C. punched me in the jaw."

Kit gasped at this revelation. Her lips gently kissed the aforementioned area. She giggled. "I'm surprised he told you where I was."

"He didn't. It took me about three hours of talking to convince Phyllis that I wasn't a heartless bastard and then she convinced K.C." Rafe eyed her sternly. "You know, if I wasn't so sure about you and me, I could be very jealous about you and K.C."

Kit shook her head, her body arching invitingly underneath him. "I think he and Phyl will get together," she told him. "In fact, he's going to bring her here next week."

"We'll let her recuperate in the guest house. She can help you with your wedding plans."

"And where will I be?"

"In the master bedroom with the master." He grinned wolfishly. "The rest of my family is winging its way home from Europe, anxiously waiting to meet you." He eyed her anxious features. "Now what's the matter?" Rafe demanded softly.

"Your parents, especially your mother, are going to be very upset about me. Family is so important to you, and my roots are decidedly muddy."

He placed his fingers across her mouth. "I know many people who have cut off their roots and started life anew. I told you before I am not ashamed of you.

And at thirty-six, I hardly think I need parental consent to get married." Rafe grinned suddenly. "I don't think I've told you about my Uncle Arthur the kleptomaniac and—"

Roughly, she pulled his head down to hers, her mouth effectively silencing him. One day she would tell him just how lonely and turbulent her life had been. But now his love and support chased away all the ugly memories.

Rafe's response was instantaneous. His mouth devoured her anxieties and doubts; his hands stroked away her fears and apprehensions. "I love you," he whispered fiercely. "You are the most important thing in the world to me. You're my life, my very soul." He bent his head, his lips gently seeking the erect nipples of her quivering breasts. His hand slid over her smooth stomach, her thighs opening to receive his exploring fingers.

Her body trembled under his passionate caresses. Her hands slid to the waistband of his jeans, her fingers finding the snap, then the zipper. She felt him shudder under his growing desire.

Rafe tossed the jeans aside, just missing the peacefully sleeping dog. "I just thought of the perfect place for our honeymoon," he announced, bracing his hands on either side of her, his eyes darkening passionately as he surveyed her shapely body. "It was the very first place I saw you."

"You want to honeymoon in the Shippleys' living

room?" Kit giggled and reached up to pull him back down on top of her.

"Hardly," he returned dryly, smiling into her liquid sapphire eyes. "It was on board the *Conquistador*, right before we set sail. I looked down and saw this mass of fiery hair shimmering under the sun and glittering with confetti and streamers. Then you looked up and I saw your beautiful face." He bent his head and kissed her deeply.

Kit looped her arms around his waist, arching her body in delightful anticipation. "I don't know. The last time I was a passenger on your ship, I spent the entire cruise flat on my back in bed." She shuddered, remembering her bout of seasickness.

Rafe leered at her, his hands raising her hips to meet the bold urgency of his passion, a wide-dimpled grin spreading over his face. "Strange," he said, "but that's exactly where you'll be spending this cruise, too."

Dell Bestsellers

- [ ] **A PERFECT STRANGER** by Danielle Steel ..$3.50 (17221-7)
- [ ] **FEED YOUR KIDS RIGHT**
  by Lendon Smith, M.D. $3.50 (12706-8)
- [ ] **THE FOUNDING** by Cynthia Harrod-Eagles ..$3.50 (12677-0)
- [ ] **GOODBYE, DARKNESS**
  by William Manchester $3.95 (13110-3)
- [ ] **GENESIS** by W.A. Harbinson $3.50 (12832-3)
- [ ] **FAULT LINES** by James Carroll $3.50 (12436-0)
- [ ] **MORTAL FRIENDS** by James Carroll $3.95 (15790-0)
- [ ] **THE HORN OF AFRICA** by Philip Caputo $3.95 (13675-X)
- [ ] **THE OWLSFANE HORROR** by Duffy Stein ..$3.50 (16781-7)
- [ ] **INGRID BERGMAN: MY STORY**
  by Ingrid Bergman and Alan Burgess $3.95 (14085-4)
- [ ] **THE UNFORGIVEN**
  by Patricia J. MacDonald $3.50 (19123-8)
- [ ] **SOLO** by Jack Higgins $2.95 (18165-8)
- [ ] **THE SOLID GOLD CIRCLE**
  by Sheila Schwartz $3.50 (18156-9)
- [ ] **THE CORNISH HEIRESS**
  by Roberta Gellis $3.50 (11515-9)
- [ ] **THE RING** by Danielle Steel $3.50 (17386-8)
- [ ] **AMERICAN CAESAR**
  by William Manchester $4.50 (10424-6)

At your local bookstore or use this handy coupon for ordering:

Dell | **DELL BOOKS**
P.O. BOX 1000, PINEBROOK, N.J. 07058

Please send me the books I have checked above. I am enclosing $ _____
(please add 75¢ per copy to cover postage and handling). Send check or money
order—no cash or C.O.D.'s. Please allow up to 8 weeks for shipment.

Mr/Mrs/Miss _____

Address _____

City _____ State/Zip _____